AM I WHAT I WANT TO BE

Prasanta Bhattacharya

Invincible Publishers

Published by
Invincible Publishers
201A, SAS Tower, Sector 38, Gurugram – 122003
Phone: +91-124-4034247, +91 9355675555
Web: www.i-publish.in

First Published in 2020

ISBN: 978-93-89600-78-0

This book is for you, Dad.
You showed me the ways to live really simple
and truly human.
Your work and effort touched many lives.
My deepest respect to you, wherever you are in heaven.

Content

Acknowledgment

With profound gratitude, I wish to thank every person who has come into my life, touched, inspired and helped me dream through their encouragement. I am grateful to my family for magnificent support and contributions to my journey and to the creation of this book. No word is enough to express my gratitude to my childhood friends for their love and wishes. I pay homage to my teachers for inspirational teachings, generously showing their wisdom, care and blessings. A big thank you to my precious friends and colleagues for their support and guidance. I am thankful to those persons whom I could not meet in person, and still they always helped me through book editing, design and formatting. Finally my deepest respect and gratitude to all those persons who inspired me through their heroics in the society and great contributions to humanity.

Introduction

My mind reminds me that I must write before it goes to sleep. We all have a lot in us through our experiences, ideas, emotions, imaginations and much more. Most of the time, they just live in the mind-box, sometimes so deep inside, that they never receive a pull to come out. Incidentally, I happened to meet and know Aakash a year back, found my day, and started writing his mind. His mind aspires to reveal his thoughts to others. After all, he represents many of us and his mind absolutely deserves to be read. You must be curious. Who is this Aakash? Why should we bother to know his thoughts?

Aakash is a middle-aged person, nothing that great about him. He is an average person, a so-called common man, still very special and different. You can feel his presence amongst many of us. His presence spreads everywhere in our society, nation, maybe even wider. Like all of us, Aakash also has been through a journey and has a lot of experience from everything that came his way. At times, his prior experience showed him the path to the future. Sometimes his past is compromised to follow the path forward. There are cases, where he has been highly successful. At times, failure brutally met him in the journey. We all are human beings. Success and failure are not alien to us!

Everyone is a guest in this beautiful world. We come here with a start and expiry date. What stays in the middle is a dream, experience, reality, hope, and much more. We all go through these phases, don't we? Every human being has a dream, maybe at different scales depending on their background and surroundings. We all chase our dreams while we continue with this journey. The great Indian cricketer, Sachin Tendulkar said, “Chase your dreams but make sure you don’t find shortcuts.” During the journey, some of us manage to steer in the right direction. Some of us struggle to follow the path and lose focus. Few of us take a pause and review where we stand. Given the dream we always had deep inside our mind, we try to find the answer of “AM I WHAT I WANTED TO BE?”

Over the years, decades, or even centuries, so many things happened on our planet. So many people have tried their best. Many societies have achieved what they wanted to achieve. Many nations rose; some much higher than the others. And they achieved it through the aspirations, they nurtured over the years with strong determination. Some nations tasted failure too while some completely collapsed and dissolved. In some cases, these people, societies, nations became what they wanted to be while in others, they became what the journey made them.

We must ask ourselves this question. We would always be happy to say, “Yes, I am what I wanted to be!”

In our journey, we experience life in our own ways. The box of experience is rich with good, bad, ugly, and beautiful experiences as they are catered to us and as we receive them. During the journey, sometimes we may get exhausted and off the track. And life goes on and on. Even former US president Barack Obama had to remind citizens in a college opportunity summit: “Now, as a nation, we don’t promise equal outcomes, but we were founded on the idea that everybody should have an equal opportunity to succeed. No matter who you are, what you look like, where you come from, you can make it. That’s an essential promise of America. Where you start should not determine where you end up.” The more we experience, the more we try to tune ourselves. And in an ever-adjusting world, we keep on moving on a path guided by response to, “Am I what I want to be?" We chose to be who we are! We chose our future! What remains is a journey, experience and memory.

The presence of Aakash is felt more on our planet during difficult days, in the form of an individual, society and nation. Let's see how the journey looks like for Aakash. I am sure, however distant we are, whatever differences we have, despite it all, many of us will be able to connect with him. Stay with me while Aakash connects with you all!

Prasanta Bhattacharya / xi

They All Started From The Same Point...

There was hardly any difference in what was happening. It was the mid-70s. It was Aakash's turn to come to this planet as a new guest. He was welcomed in a small village in the eastern part of India. This village was green all over with trees everywhere, rivers flowing with lushness and fields covered with fresh air. Every season had something special to offer the villagers. Be it the shadow of the mango trees during hot summers or the small tea stall under the tile roof on a boring rainy day. It could be burning wood giving warmth to people in the early mornings of cold foggy winters. People had enough reasons to assemble and gossip. Most of the population were either farmers or daily labors. Some had money from their businesses and few educated fellows were engaged in government jobs. The roads were still far from the black tar. The houses were built of mud and straw. Drainage was being handled naturally by ponds.

People knew each other. Be it for reasons good or bad, there were always people around you. They were ready to help each other. Believe me, too much attachment at times even created problems for each other. All these were parts of their day to day lives. There was hardly any means of transportation that could take you through 12 kilometers distance in 30 minutes. One bus used to run once every two hours. Of course, there was no traffic congestion. Neither could you hear honks nor would inhale any smoke in the air. People used to commute even on the roof of the bus. There were tube wells in each locality. Women used to come in queues and take drinking water back home. Washrooms lay under the sky if there was a bush to hide behind. There was a single hospital in the village. People used to call it the primary health centre. The designated pharmacist used to provide red and yellow tablets. Those tablets used to work well, whatever the sickness was. The village adjusted to the darkness as electricity seldom gave them a chance to celebrate. At night, few houses had electrical lights. For majority of the villagers, kerosene was the source of light.

There were primary, secondary, and higher secondary schools. The school infrastructure was not that great. But the school ambience was good enough to learn. There was no private school in the village then. Everyone had to come to these schools for their early education. Those days, there was no admission test. There were a few small grocery shops in the entire village. Most of the day to day needs were available there. Every day there was a special market under the sky, in the open air. And every Saturday and Sunday, the market used to be even more ceremonial. People used to shop, spend some time with friends and known ones at the roadside shops with a cup of tea. You could be lucky enough to get an invitation, in case your friend had bought good fish or mutton. No hurry to buy a gift! Only a box of sweets would do!

Media and entertainment were still there. There is no reason to think that people did not have these elements in life there. It is just that people did not have a lot of real-time updates. People could not dream of comfortable and convenient means of entertainment. Of course, there was no mobile phone, no internet, and no laptop at that time. There was a post office – the one means of communication which brightened people's day. People were so excited when they used to hear the 'ting tong' alarm of the bicycle that the postman used to ride. The postman was one of the closest people in their regular lives. Any news – good or bad – could come through this postman only. Not just a letter, there were telegrams and money orders as well for the people. Very few families had that small black and white television that existed at that time. All neighbors used to come to the house of these few families to watch the TV programs. They used to watch movies, soccer and cricket world cups. It was quite a get-together of families in front of those few TV stations. Anywhere in the village you move to, you would hear the news coming from the radio. Old people would sleep but still not switch off the radio. Once a year, there used to be a movie show in the panchayat ground. People from nearby villages used to come, sit on the ground, and watch the movies.

There were a lot of Hindu temples in the village. People used to celebrate the festivals of all religions. During the times of *Sarodiya, Eid, Diwali, Holi, Sarasvati Puja, Charak Puja*, all of these used to be celebrated together with new clothes, food, and fun. Not that everyone had the same scale of celebration, but it was very much inclusive in society, regardless of whatever little differences there were amongst people. Everyone's relatives came to the village during those days. Post celebration, the village used to go back to being silent and dark waiting for the next celebration.

Aakash had his childhood education in this village. The teachers were very dedicated. They nurtured each child as their own and treated them to the best of their abilities. They were their guides and mentors. Students had high respect for their teachers. At the same time, they feared them as well. Besides the syllabus, they spent a lot of time together, be it in the school corridor, teacher's room or the playground. The teachers were role models for their children. They used to inspire students and taught them to set larger goals in life. They showed them the path to follow their dreams. For students, it is important to learn the subject at hand. But the teachers made them even think beyond the subject. They used to discuss happenings around the world, advancements in science, socio-economic health of the region, and the impact of good or bad politics in society. Students had a lot of emphasis on studies, sports, and cultural events. The teachers helped them to build their mindsets to work in a team, contribute to various aspects of life. Despite being a small place with no posh infrastructures, learning was limitless. Aakash was fortunate to have those teachers in his early life. He could see the world through their eyes.

During his primary classes, the students used to distribute government-funded bread and clothes to the fellow students. Aakash still remembers how the teachers brought confidence in them. The teachers used to ask a few students to summarize learning from the session. It was a privilege to share his learning with the entire class. During Saraswati Puja, they used to organize an event. There used to be an intra-school football tournament. Aakash still feels proud to be a part of the winning school. All the students used to go to the next village to support their own school team. How many times in life do we see people coming to a field to support their teams after travelling 8 kilometers on foot? How many times do you get a chance to stand in a queue on 15th August to hear the headmaster address to the students followed by a few candies? How many times did you get an opportunity to serve food to all your friends during *Saraswati puja*? How many times did you feel happy even after getting punishment to help your friends in an examination who were not as good as you were in studies? The African proverb says it all, "It takes a village to raise a child."

Childhood Shapes The Future...

Whenever Aakash thinks of his childhood, his friends always take the center-stage in his life. They were together, almost all the time, they were awake. Besides school hours, they used to spend long time in the pond, and in the playground. Be it swimming, football, cricket, it was very competitive, but still so friendly. They loved each other, they fought with each other, and more importantly, they taught each other. They had enough reasons to laugh together and cry together. Togetherness was such an integral part of their lives. It was not easy to dream in difficult times when comfort was at its lowest. But they could do it as they had faith in each other.

His family had always been supportive to Aakash. Through his family, Aakash could see all the beauties in his early childhood. Family is that important aspect in life which teaches us to love our village, people, respect our teachers, fellow citizens and help our friends. Aakash was born in a joint family with a brother and sister. His father had always been the simplest person in his life. The people used to respect his father as a great teacher. His mother did everything to see her children happy. In a poor family, a mother absorbs most of the pain to see her children smile. Besides parents and siblings, there were his grandmother, uncle, and aunty. His family had a strong educational backbone. It's not that they had all the happiness in the world. Rather they had all the elements of life – challenges and accomplishments, all in one box.

Aakash is now in his mid-40's; he hardly gets time to walk on those childhood paths. At times, he sits in the balcony of his apartment in the city. Through the light and dark shades on the roads, his mind goes back to those roads and the path to his village. He can still visualize his house in the village. The silent road at night still waits for his arrival. The school bell calls him to attend the classes. His mind still wants to play with childhood friends. He is still excited about the *Saraswati Puja*. He wants to meet his teachers and get their blessings. At night, he still misses his grandmother's stories.

This does not mean that all were only pleasant memories. There were conflicts and fights too in the locality. For small things, people used to quarrel. Some people used to torture the ones who were not so privileged. However, in the long run, Aakash still has a good picture in mind and that's what he wants to continue to cherish with. Our life is just time slices. Aakash keeps the good slices on the top of his memory.

If we consider our life as a journey and its time slices as milestones, people around us are our co-passengers. People have a long-lasting impression on our journey. Through these people, we get the taste of our experiences. Aakash had many living beings around him during childhood.

It was a full house with grandmother, parents, uncle, aunty, brothers and sisters. It will be unfair if we don't speak about 'Tommy', Aakash's beloved dog at home. Aakash brought Tommy home when Tommy was just a month old and Aakash was 7 years old. Everyone in the family initially went against the idea of having a dog at home. That day, somehow Tommy fell from little Aakash's hands and started crying. That incident created a lot of sympathy at home and suddenly, he became everyone's favorite 'Tommy'. Aakash's father started buying dog's soap, feeding bottle, and milk for Tommy. On a winter day, when Tommy was in the *verandah* and started crying in cold at night, Aakash took him to the bedroom. Gradually from the floor of the bedroom, he got into the bed and since then, started sleeping with Aakash in all seasons till Aakash moved to college.

Aakash still remembers how he and his sister used to wake up at midnight and fed Tommy the needed milk. Tommy became his all-time friend. A lot of times, Tommy was the only creature in the world with whom Aakash could share his emotions and feelings. Canadian novelist, Heather O'Neill wrote in her debut novel, "Becoming a child again is what is impossible. That's what you have a legitimate reason to be upset over. Childhood is the most valuable thing that's taken away from you in life, if you think about it."

Family And Friends Are Big Influencers...

Aakash was very fortunate to have his grandmother at home. She was more than sixty when Aakash was just five years old. Her grandmother was not that educated, but she had all the knowhow of this little planet. Aakash used to listen to stories from his grandmother. His grandmother had the habit of always keeping the radio switched on. Aakash also used to listen to some of those radio programs. She liked rice with milk and every day, she used to keep some portion of food aside for little Aakash. Aakash used to spend a long time in the pond, swimming with his friends. He was very fond of playing football and cricket. Sometimes, he used to get wounded. For such problems, her grandmother was his first doctor. During the examination times, every morning, she used to wake him up at 5 AM, and prepare a cup of tea for Aakash. Aakash did not have a choice other than reading his books after having the tea. Whenever Aakash did anything wrong, he knew his grandmother would stand beside him to protect him. At the same time, she would tell him later, what was right and what was not. In such a remote village, her grandmother was like a guiding light for him during his childhood.

Aakash is now a father of fourteen years old young boy. Many times, his interaction with his son reminds him of his father. His father studied in the village and later had his higher education in City College in Kolkata.

He was a Master of Arts in both, English and History. He was fond of music and food. He was a teacher in another village with the majority of people from so-called backward classes. His father used to go to school every Monday and return home on Saturday. Be it summer, winter, or rainy season, he was never absent in the school. It was not an easy task for his father to set up the government school there and encourage people to send their children to school. The villagers also used to respect him a lot for his contribution there.

Aakash did not have the opportunity to spend a long time with his father because of his father's weekly schedule. Sunday was always eventful with his father, be it reading newspaper in the morning, or going to saloon, which was beside the road, under the sky, sitting on the bricks; or spending time in the market to buy vegetables or fish. It used to be a great lunch on every Sunday at home. During the evenings, Aakash and his siblings used to listen to his father's college life story.

Sometimes, his father used to take him to his school. Aakash used to get a grand welcome there. After all, he was the headmaster's youngest son and who else can have better privilege than Aakash in his father's own school? In a middle-class family, it gives a lot of pride and pleasure for having such attention. Aakash's father never sat with him during studies.

But he injected in his mind, the importance of being successful and being a good human being.

While his father used to be busy with his school, the home front used to be managed by his mother. His mother struggled a lot managing a big joint family with so small income. With a smiling face and determined mind, she had managed the kitchen over the years. After a lot of debates and fights with Aakash's father, she used to get the budget for the Puja season. Aakash was very reluctant to face the urban life. His mother always used to put him in front, be it in the train, be it in the shop in a city. His mother wanted him to forget any weakness and focus on the future.

His mother was not that educated, and she could not help her children in their studies. But all through her life, whatever she did, she did for the children. When Aakash was just nine years old, he got to know that his mother was diagnosed with a critical illness. It was a big blow to Aakash and his family. They spent countless nights without sleep, thinking of their mother's health condition and praying for her recovery. With time, we may get a lot of things in life. But you would never get mother's love from anyone else in your lifetime. His mother wanted her children to be educated and self-sufficient. Having been from a remote village, adjusting with other privileged people and having a similar social life is not an easy struggle. His mother taught him to face the world as it came on the way. His first experience of riding a bus or train, walking on a suburban railway station, or crossing the busy roads in a city – all came with catching her mother's hand.

On every step Aakash walked in his childhood, there was anxiety, fear of unknowns, disappointment for not being able to buy something in a city store, or for being ignored by his urban relatives. Aakash understands that there was never a better option that his parents could offer him at that time. Through a brutal reality, he had learnt how to face challenges in difficult times, and he learnt that from his mother.

Aakash was fortunate to have his brother and sister during his golden childhood. His brother was six years older than Aakash and sister was 3 years older. Having been the youngest in family, Aakash had immense love from everyone. He considers his elder brother as the most intelligent person he has ever met. He was widely respected in the village as a good student and a good human being. He was Aakash's childhood idol.

Aakash spent memorable time with his brother, be that in the playground or at home. During the football match, he and his elder brother used to be in the opponent teams. His brother was merciless in tackling him hard on the ground. They used to challenge each other hard during the matches. And the same brother used to take care of Aakash's injury when they returned home. It's great to have such a brother at home whom you can follow, from whom you get inspiration.

When Aakash had a tough time in solving science or mathematics problems, his brother taught him in an easy manner. His brother had the passion of researching at home on light, electricity, magnetism and mechanics. His brother had loads of talent that a normal student doesn't usually have. In his childhood, his brother would take Aakash to the shop or market, hand over the heavy bag to him and then leave the duty to little Aakash. Aakash never minded. He knew his brother was just like that. Maybe, all great brothers are like that only.

In not so advanced village life, children go through a lot of trauma. While they do get fresh air and a lot of other great stuff, there are problems as well. Fellow people fight with each other for nothing. A peaceful life can get into fire suddenly. In a middle-class family, parents usually stay busy with their day-to-day stuff. They may not have enough time to spend with their kids. Aakash's sister was very worried about him. What did Aakash do in the school? Was anyone beating Aakash? Was Aakash learning to face the future? Would Aakash do well in studies? Even, would Aakash get a wife, having such a small height?

A sister is a sister, always next to our mother! His sister always had an eye on him, fearing her brother could be exposed to anything wrong in life. They used to share the egg during dinner. She used to influence Aakash's friends so that they would protect her brother. Two brothers and a sister formed a small 'home' inside the home. They used to dance together. Three of them used to play cricket with a few of their other friends. Trust me, his sister was never behind. Don't think everything was all rosy. There were struggles, challenges as well! But they had faced them together. Maybe, challenges bonded them better. It's a god's gift to have brother and sister like Aakash had.

In our childhood, we need someone to be afraid of with great respect. His uncle was a very strong personality. He was very fit, well maintained person with a very clear philosophy of being honest, talking straight and doing things himself. He never shouted at Aakash or his siblings and still they were all very afraid of him. You can't do anything wrong in your childhood, as long as you have such an uncle at home. Every month he used to give some pocket money to Aakash and his siblings. That little money was so important and useful those days. During the evening, Aakash and his siblings had to study just because his uncle would have come home anytime from his office. Respect with fear or fear with respect were important building blocks in our characters. His aunty came to the village post marriage. Coming from a city she adjusted herself in the village with a big smile. In short time, she became everyone's best friend in the family. Her ability to welcome everyone was unparalleled. Her presence at home always brought in a sense of togetherness. Then Aakash got his cousin brother and sister. Finally he had a brother and sister at home to whom he was bit senior. At times aunts from father and mother sides used to come their house with cousins. It used to be great gathering with lots of play and fun.

Childhood cannot be complete without friends. Aakash's friends were not from that established families. Rather, they were mostly uneducated; financially they were lagging too. Most of them even did not have meals twice. Their parents used to work as daily laborers. Their physical built and strength were their skillset and proficiency. The surroundings were so off the mark, even Aakash and his family seemed way ahead in terms of financial status, social prestige in the locality. In such situations, where people had so many challenges, it was very difficult to focus on friendship and bonding. As Bengali poet Sukanta Bhattacharya said, "The hungry world is all prose, even the round full moon looks like a roasted piece of bread".

Even with all these odds, their childhood friendships were cemented rock solid. At that stage, there was no greed, no expectation. Aakash had the first important lesson in life at this stage – "You may be underprivileged; you may not have books to read; meal twice a day may be a big reward; having a soft bed may sound like a luxury; but if you have genuine friendship, love and affection, you can overcome all these odds!"

Many 'first time' things happen in our life during this time. We can never forget the magical moment when one goes to school alone for the first time. How can we forget the day when one rides a bicycle for the first time? There are moments of a great sense of accomplishment when your hands wave through water for the first time while swimming. The sound of "A for Apple, B for Boy..." still resonates in our ears.

Aakash got into the flow of life like many others. There were a lot of learnings. They had challenges, but family and friends together showed the promises of future. Maybe, they had very few avenues of pride and pleasures, and that reality had brought their families and friends close to each other. Sometimes worst brings best out of us! John Calvin Maxwell, an American author wrote, "Family and friendships are two of the greatest facilitators of happiness."

Gear Up To Teenage... Teachers Inspire...

Then came the time when all the friends moved to secondary school. All went there, taking with them, the basic learning from childhood. New faces came and joined them. There was a variety of students with all shades of characters. There were new classrooms, new teachers and staff. Their learning spheres started expanding and so was the pressure of focusing more on the future. Physical activity and interest in sports increased. They got new friends as well as new competitions. The School hour was between 11 am to 4 pm. Rest of the time, they were either at private tuitions or with friends or family. They used to come home only during mealtime.

Between Class V to XII, our mental and physical characters build up. Some teachers took extra care of the students. Besides studies, those teachers spent additional time with the students in discussing current affairs, motivating them to have dreams for success. Aakash was fortunate to have some of the great teachers and good friends who gave him a lot of encouragement to do more, to shine better. The founder of the Republic of Turkey, Kemal Atatürk reflected long back, "A good teacher is like a candle – it consumes itself to light the way for others."

Aakash understood that he was being treated differently. He just couldn't have ended up being an ordinary, self-centric person. He thought, he must stand up and create a positive impact in his surroundings. Everyone wanted to support him and see Aakash successful. And that drove Aakash to set wider goals for himself. This was the time when Aakash started sharing his mind with fellow friends. His thinking for others, willingness to help, energy to spend time with others – All were very special for his friends. Sometimes, it is important we share our feelings and dreams with others. This helps us to stay on track of what we intend to head on. More importantly, this sets an unseen benchmark and path to our own life.

This was the time when they could not think of not seeing each other even for a single day. This was the time when they started dreaming for the future– a dream to change the society, dream to leave positive impressions on lives, dream to bring smiles to hundreds of faces. They did not have a hundred rupees note in their pockets. Neither they had a car or bungalow, nor did they have a corporate life. Still, they dreamt big at that time.

This was the time when Aakash and his friends started a small cricket association in their village. This was the time, they arranged for movies to set up a library room in their village. This was the time they used to go to flood-impacted rural areas with food, medicines, and other help. There were many more such times, all added to their priceless lifetime experiences. Today, Aakash wonders, how could they do it with so many odds in life? Answer is simple – in their friend circle, there was no individualistic life that time. Answer is easy – there was no difference, no ego, and no race amongst the friends.

Like the river in the village, Aakash experienced both tides in life – sometimes, high and sometimes, low. He never stopped dreaming in his life. He made his path only forward; whatever obstacles came on the way. He did not compromise with his life and beliefs, ever. He played, studied, spent time with friends. He was never ready to miss any single opportunity to mingle with others. Aakash was so concerned about his friends that he was always prepared to make an individual sacrifice to keep his friends a little bit ahead. His friends did the same as well.

There were funny incidents as well. Many times, Aakash and his friends stole coconuts from their own gardens. They thought, it was better for the friends to get caught by their own parents, rather than by others and get beaten! What a logic! Affection was never just one-sided. His friends loved and supported each other a lot. They never questioned each other, when one had asked for any help or favor.

During this time, Aakash and his friends realized that their society was not so bonded. In fact, their seniors used to quarrel with each other on small things. This was when they had planned to celebrate two major festivals in an organized manner in the society; one was *Laxmi Puja* (worshipping the goddess of wealth) and another, was *Holi* (festival of colors). The whole society used to celebrate these two festivals together. Leaving all differences aside, they used to transform into a single family on these days. Their neighborhood uncle who usually had never talked to them throughout the year, would come forward and arrange for the cooking logistics himself. Aakash still wonders, what could pull that uncle to these events? Was that the magic of togetherness?

The whole society used to cook and have food together for those few days. This may not be a big thing today in modern housing. However, thirty years back, in a remote village, bringing everyone on the same platform and sharing the fun and celebrating together, was a great feeling of accomplishment. Today, Aakash wonders, how could they do it with so many divided people in the society? Answer is simple – their friend circle used to think and care for each other. They could bring in a sense of belongingness in the society!

Journey To The Future...

Aakash did well in his studies and moved to one of the renowned engineering colleges in his state. He opted for the Mining Engineering course. Entry to this college opened a much wider window in Aakash's life. Many bright students from different parts of the state came here for studies. Aakash got new friends and life in college brought in wings of freedom. Background and wavelength of connections silently brought the primary group of friends together. The college campus was simply awesome! The infrastructure offered a wide range of facilities to the students. Many structures on the campus were built during the British era. The clock tower, the main building, the director's club, canteen, hostels, playgrounds, the road beside the graveyard, lakes inside the campus gradually became part of daily living.

Hostel life was very fun-filled. Students used to have food together, go out together, watch movies together. Suddenly, the mess staff also became very close and important ones in their lives. The common room was another attraction, be it for watching a cricket match on big television, or playing carrom or table tennis. Togetherness was the key in life at that time. They used to go for vocational training/workshops once every year. Life brought all shades of colors to them. Friendship found new meanings of living. There were hope and dream in every corner of the campus. And anxiety had its own place too. A dream got the wings and got magnified as Aakash found his dream partner, Camellia from his own village. Every weekend Aakash used to come to the village from his college hostel. Aakash's childhood friends also were busy with their own lives, at work, or their colleges. A couple of educated friends went to nearby colleges and not so educated ones stepped out for jobs and livelihoods. This is the juncture when a person's life gradually moves to a different orbit. Maybe this is the law of life as sketched by GOD himself! You leave behind something and move on with something new. Suddenly one realizes he or she has transitioned into a man or woman. Their perspective and outlook towards life find an extended horizon.

It was that period in Aakash's life when love did not understand any barrier. Life seemed to be very colorful and there were always plenty of dreams in the mind. With the new love in his life, the share of dreams increased. Because of little things, they felt unbearable pain a day and the next day when they met again, it was as if everything was reborn in life. This is the time, one does not do everything based on a reason, or with an expectation. Things just happen, because you do what you enjoy. Aakash is fortunate to have someone, so committed all through his life.

This was the time, Aakash's father had retired from his job. This was the time, Aakash's brother and sister moved on to their new lives post jobs and marriages. This was the time, his grandmother, uncle, aunty and cousins moved to a new home in the city. This was the time, Aakash lost his 'best' friend Tommy forever. This was the time, childhood friends gradually moved on to their own lives. The old teachers became just a memory, as time passed by. This was the time, Aakash experienced how a large, united and loving family gradually shrunk to a small lonely unit. Everywhere it was just memories, and Aakash's heart just kept on searching them everywhere without success.

This was the time, Aakash got his brother in law and sister in law. They showed Aakash the importance of hard work and strong determination in their careers.

This was also the time when new college friends knocked on life's door. This was the time; his ladylove came to bring in new purpose to his life. The great Albert Einstein had told us long back, "Life is like riding a bicycle. To keep your balance, you must keep moving."

Very soon, Aakash realized, "Change is the only constant in life". He knew he must move on. In around the first 20 years of his life, he, himself had set a benchmark for his own life. It must not end up just seeing the dreams. It was now his turn to make them a reality. It was just not about becoming an engineer. It was just not about being part of a wider friend network. It was just not about helping others to imagine their futures. He just couldn't be complacent with this. He knew very well he must do much more to achieve what he always had aspired for. In the last two years of his academic life, he balanced his life with family, friends, life partner, college and career goal. He made every attempt to excel in all these areas.

Getting a job was very crucial at this stage. That was another beginning of a long journey into the future. Unfortunately, the job market in India towards the end of the last century was not that great. Information technology was just coming up. Manufacturing, production industries were slowing down. Having been a mining engineer, Aakash had a tough time to penetrate in the mining industry. He kept on preparing better and tried all possible places to see if he could make an entry and start his career. Some of his friends got jobs and they all used to celebrate their success in the hostel. Aakash knew his turn would come one day. And finally, Aakash made it one day. He got a job offer from a mining company. Every- one got relieved, thinking the struggle had finally come to an end. Then a day came when Aakash had to say 'bye' to his college. After a few days, he packed up his bag to travel to his job location. All the people, memories were left behind with an unknown journey into the future.

Mann Ki Baat (Inner Thoughts)...

It was mid-summer in India. Aakash was all set for a new journey. The climate was very humid, and the scorching sunlight was doing its best to suck all the energy from inside. Still, it was his dear Kolkata; the city of joy! There were thousands of people all over the railway station. Aakash bought a newspaper, took a cup of tea and found his seat in the 3-tier coach on the window side. While he was busy in settling down, an aged person came along with his young daughter. The old gentleman checked with Aakash if they were in the right train and right coach. Aakash noticed another mid-aged person was already lying on the topmost berth listening to music on his mobile. Aakash took his seat and started focusing on the newspaper. The train was expected to start in another 10 minutes.

In the meantime, many vendors came inside the coach for selling food. Some came for selling old books and magazines. Through the narrow and crowded passage in the coach, a young man came inside with heavy luggage and his mother followed him. While the young man was keeping his luggage on the side upper berth, his mother was relaxed after taking the side lower berth. Aakash understood six of them had already occupied their seats. The train was about to leave. Just when he was thinking if the other two people would come or not, he noticed that two aged gentlemen came in the coach. One seemed to be very sophisticated and well-dressed formal person in his late forties. Another person was a bit senior and seemed to be a very serious looking person. In a while, all of them settled down. The train finally started. One...two...three, first few stations left behind in few minutes. In the first one hour or so, everyone was busy with their breakfasts and then switched their attention to mobile phones or laptops. Some of these co-passengers updated their nearest ones that the train had started on time!

Aakash was looking outside, through the window. He was eagerly waiting to cross the station of his native place. The bridge on the river reminded him it was about to come. He could smell that old known place. In a while, the train crossed that station as well. Before Aakash could go down the memory lane, the young lady on his side introduced herself. Gradually Aakash got to know all of them. The person on the top berth was a gold businessman, going to Hyderabad after a week of break from Kolkata. On the side berths, the young man was a student and his mother a professor in one of the best universities in Kolkata. The young lady was an engineering professional and her father was a retired private farm employee. The suited, booted person was a mid-level executive in a corporate house and going to Vizag. And the last person who was giving an update to his family every hour was a central government officer. Aakash also introduced himself to his co-passengers.

After a while, the old retired person asked Aakash, "Can I read your newspaper, if you don't mind?" Aakash obliged and passed on the paper.

The gentleman with a cool expression had his spectacle on. After glancing through the first page, he kept on talking with sarcasm, "All international leaders are now coming to India. We are now a global power. And see the young generation! They are struggling to get jobs. Even if they get one, not sure how long they can even retain it. Here is my daughter. I spent all my savings on her engineering study. She studied well, got a job. After a year, management suddenly said, she is no longer needed. Now I am taking her to Hyderabad for finding a new job. While people like me are banking on interest from small savings for healthcare affordability, new generation like my daughter's is experiencing job crisis and lack of job security in the absence of appropriate labor law."

The young lady was a bit embarrassed. She whispered to her father, "Daddy, what's the point in telling all these? There are jobs, but only the best will secure them. It is survival of the fittest."

The lady in her early fifties on the side lower berth was listening so far. Before Aakash could say anything, she reacted, "My daughter, what 'best' are you talking about? More than talent, caste matters." She continued pointing to her son on the side upper berth, "This is my son. He did well in his engineering entrance examination. His rank was good in the national level merit list. Yet he could not secure his branch of choice. Everywhere there is quota, quota, quota... So much of discrimination and reservation everywhere! Now, I am taking my son to Bhubaneswar for admission in a private engineering college. Thank God, we saved some money for his higher studies!"

The young man said, "Mom, it is ok to study in a private college. It's ok if I don't get a chance in a government college. There is no infrastructure, freedom, no progressive thoughts in those government colleges. Nor there is any security. Remember last year, you were a bit sympathetic and supportive of the students when they were staging a peaceful campaign to save democracy on the college campus. Did you forget what had happened to you later? All those political cadres came to our house at midnight and literally threatened us for life. When we went to the police station, they even did not want to take the complaint."

Aakash was truly out of words, struggling with how to ease up the situation. The corporate person closed his laptop and commented, "I understand what all you are going through. No one is secure in this generation. I am working in a corporate house. All through my life, I have worked hard to manage our living. But midway of my career, I see all my money is going to tax. I understand that more we earn; more the income tax is. That's the norm everywhere in the world. But what is disappointing is that our hard-earned money is being used by the government, but we don't have any social security. When we are thrown out of the job, the government does not even think of us. All our income tax contribution is forgotten. Why can't we assess how this is handled in the developed countries? Everywhere social security benefit is calculated based on the years of working tenure and one's contribution through income tax. Only in India, we, the salaried people in private firms are so royally ignored."

The central government officer was silent so far. He now took the turn. He told the corporate person, "You are talking about social security? At least senior employees like me will get some pension. New joiners won't even get that. Tell me, where is our money going? All these things are happening because of corruption. Everywhere it is corruption. Do you know where I am heading to at this age? My family is in Kolkata; my children are still attending their high schools. I work for the election commission. Last year, I was posted in a rural area. I tried my best to stop rigging. I stood up against those political leaders and cadres to enable common people to cast their votes of choice. And you know what reward I received? I am now transferred to Andhra Pradesh, to another remote place. What's the point in standing up for democracy? You and your family only suffer and there is no end to it."

The gold businessman was almost sleeping. He woke up and smiled. He asked a vendor to give samosa to everyone. He came down from the top berth and sat on the lower berth and said, "I know you all are very educated. I could not study much. I went to Hyderabad when I was just twenty, with a small job in a gold shop. Now I have my own business. I don't understand what you are discussing. You must be knowing many things. But I realize one thing. This surge in gold price is impacting my business. There is hardly any customer these days to buy gold."

Meanwhile, the train stopped at a long junction station. Aakash could see through the window, there were hundreds of 'coolies' staging protest on the station platform in demand for better wages. An aged tea seller came inside the coach. While he was pouring tea in those mud cups, he was talking to himself, "Protest…. Who cares? I also used to do all these trade unions when I was young. Our leaders said this is our democratic right. What happened? Nothing changed. Trust me, nothing will ever change. No one will think of the poor. At least, if we work hard now, our children will get some food; they will go to school. We could not do anything in our lives. But they will have better lives one day!"

Aakash was speechless. In a hurry, he sipped hot tea. For a while, he stopped looking at anyone. He understood there were many problems around us. But looking at these faces in the train, he understood people were having their points of view. He was hopeful that someday things would change for better. These common people would bring in the change. He remembered the famous saying, "Of the people; by the people; for the people…" If this is the *"Mann ki Baat"* of our countrymen, the government and the leaders would have no other choice but take care of its people. The train kept on running through the lines!

Democracy is a journey. We will always have different shades of people. You will have experience, opinions. There will be support, protest as well. At times people may be frustrated if their basic rights are not protected. Whom to complain? It is our democracy, people's democracy. If people suffer, they will raise their voices. It is just a matter of time and only time. People I met in the train represent us. Each of them is fighting for their rights. They will adjust to some extent if the situations demand. But never mind, they have their own limits of absorption.

Time To Build The Career...

It was a moonlit night amid a hilly place, all surrounded by silence at night. One could only hear the noise from a running compressor machine. He was sitting on a bench under the starry sky. He remembered what great APJ Abdul Kalam had said, "Look at the sky. We are not alone. The whole universe is friendly to us and conspires only to give the best to those who dream and work." There were hardly few workers on the ground. Aakash had a good time to speak to himself. This place was very remote and far off from the so-called civilization. Aakash came here along with his five other college mates. They were put into a mines housing community for the executives. Every day, Aakash used to come by company bus, from his residence to the mine. The journey was of just twenty minutes and would stay in your mind forever. The roads were like waves in the sea and your body could sense it all through the journey. Dust would love to touch you, coming through the wide-open broken window of the bus. It was a Monday-to-Saturday office schedule. Aakash liked to work in the mine as there was a lot to learn there. The mine was truly a model-like in the metal mining field in India. You got to see a lot of technical aspects of mining here, be it, approach strategy to mine face, ore transport, roof support system or the pumping mechanism to pull water from 90-meter-deep inside the mine.

This was where Aakash met one of his most respectful professional heroes; at his fifties, he was the Deputy General Manager of the mine. Aakash used to follow him from a distance, very closely. Aakash was simply stunned by his impressive personality; the way he used to stay connected to ground level, the style he used to apply with labor, executives, and other non-technical staff. Even at this age, he used to go down the mine by ladder. He had knowledge of everything that used to happen inside the mine. Aakash used to observe how much respect the miners had for this gentleman and at the same time, they had a lot of fear, in case super boss caught them sitting idle and not contributing.

The mining industry in India is a very different place, and difficult as well. As an executive, you need to work with most of the uneducated laborers. They are strong, handy and very knowledgeable, but one needs to have the key to unlock their potential to perform. As an executive, you need to exhibit a strong personality. You need to stay with them when needed, and still maintain a finely calibrated distance. You need to join hands with them when needed, but as an executive, you must show you are helping them by going above and beyond. You need to have the practical knowledge to maintain your lead status. Aakash had noticed all these qualities in his DGM. Aakash used to find all opportunities to stay connected to this old but strong man.

Sometimes, you might have gone through a struggling time in life, but that makes you mature, wiser, and stronger. Given the childhood background of Aakash, he always had a natural way of mixing with not so privileged class. His simple, down to earth style made him acceptable to the miners. He used to learn drilling and blasting from the laborers. He made his hands dirty with most of the underground mining activities. Gradually, he started becoming a confident mining engineer. Outside work, Aakash and his friends had a lot of fun at the weekend. Sometimes, they used to visit a nearby dam which was a picture-like place, covered with greenery all over. Back in the company quarter, they used to cook food themselves. Saturday night was full of fun amid the dark and silent tribal village. This was the time, Aakash's father decided to build a new house. Now they would have got a concrete house to stay. Everyone in the family was so excited. Lots of planning and budgeting discussions happened. Aakash's mother and maternal uncle worked very hard to make this possible. One person, Aakash was very closely attached to, was his maternal uncle. He was more like one of his best friends. He was his courage, mental support, the most available helping hand in any type of crisis in his life. One thing that Aakash seldom got to see in others, was his maternal uncle's willingness and commitment to help others. Life brings challenges to us at times, and with a surprise. Although everything was going well, the company had a financial crisis and for many months, employees worked without pay. Some of his friends started leaving the organization to find better opportunities somewhere else. It was a difficult time and Aakash had to take a practical decision. He wanted to move on a path that could be more forward-looking. What should Aakash do? Finally, he and one of his friends decided to leave and try for their fortune in the Information Technology industry.

Then one day he and his friend left the mine for Kolkata with an eye on the unknown future. Aakash still did not know whom to meet first after reaching Kolkata. How would he tell his parents that he was leaving a known mining job with an eye on unknown information technology field? On his way back home, Aakash asked his friend what would happen to him. His friend showed him a person on the railway platform, who did not have legs and was still managing for his living through begging. His friend said, "We must feel fortunate and thankful to the almighty GOD that we are at least in better shape than this person." Aakash realized what his friend meant, and he never forgot this lesson in his life. Many times, we crib for the misery we are into. We don't realize there are others who are suffering even more than us. If we have the right intent, there is always something that GOD has given us to pass through.

The Road Of Life Has Ups And Downs...

The situation at home was not that bad as Aakash had thought of. His father reluctantly agreed to his decision. His parents tried their best to enable their youngest son to live his dream. Aakash took admission in a software training center. His pocket was obviously very light those days. His sister helped him a lot through mental support, encouragement and financial assistance. Aakash took up this course very seriously and gave his best to gain knowledge. Meanwhile, he tried at multiple places for a job but could not secure one in the first six months.

More it got delayed; more pressure was building up! In his circle, he was known as an engineer and that also from a reputed college in India. But after one year of passing out from the college, he was back to no man's land. It was really time with a major identity crisis. In difficult times, one loses confidence; the dear ones suspect your ability; the distant ones look for every opportunity to demean you. Aakash did not let his hope go. More he struggled, better he prepared for the future. After a number of failed attempts, Aakash finally got into a job. He was thrilled to receive the offer letter from HR. His closed ones were so happy to see Aakash back on track. When someone takes a decision to change, struggles to settle down, and finally reaches the goal, it gives so much pleasure! Time teaches us a lot. We are tested for our patience and perseverance.

At around the same time, Aakash's maternal uncle got married and moved to the city for fortune. They could not celebrate the success moment together. Sometimes when you achieve something, and you find that your best friend is not around, you feel like something is missing. Sometimes, we don't realize what life gives us during our journey and what all are taken back with the passage of time.

From a hard rock mining field, Aakash landed into the software industry. He was surrounded by some of the brightest minds around him. Life was much more polished here. Knowledge and analytical minds were rewarded more than anyone else. Aakash found some good friends and colleagues in his first Information Technology job. He was mentored by the few bests of the technical leads. He and his colleagues made the workplace a real fun. Everyone loved challenges and together, they built a winning team. This was the time when the peers had a competition to learn more. But they never felt as if they were in a race. They had fresh minds to focus just on work. Promotion and rating were important, but they never snatched peace out of their minds.

Interestingly, Aakash still did not have a mobile phone. A mobile phone was still for the privileged class. The cost was still much higher for his income group. This was the time, Aakash used to stay on rent in Kolkata. The landlord was poor, but he and his family were very cordial to Aakash.

Every Friday night, Aakash used to go to his native place and come back to the office on Monday morning. The weekend was fun and eventful. Aakash used to meet his friends. He could spend long hours with Camellia. Life got back its color and Aakash started cherishing every moment.

The first one year vanished just like that. Finally, Aakash married Camellia. A long-known journey had finally come to an unknown station now. Aakash's parents happily welcomed Camellia to home. Camellia also gave her best to take care of Aakash's parents. It was a very happy family. Aakash's office was 70 kilometers away from home. He continued to stay in the rented apartment and come to meet his family in the weekend.

Life kept on moving. Office work started building up. Camellia was also expecting more time, especially after a new marriage. It was too much for Aakash to handle at the age of twenty-six! Life is not always that rosy as we tend to imagine. That's the beauty of life. One day you could feel happy for a small thing. The next day, for an even smaller thing, you may feel broken. It is important we face life as it comes to us. Neither happy moments stay forever, nor do bad days bother you permanently. Through our experiences, we learn to balance across many emotional segments of life. Then one day, the news finally came. Aakash was about to become a father. Aakash and Camellia started counting the days!

Aakash's father asked him to take Camellia to Kolkata, closer to his office. He wanted to ensure the needed medical assistance for Camellia during this critical juncture. Aakash accepted the suggestion and moved to Kolkata along with Camellia. First time Aakash felt he had really grown up!

This was the time, Aakash's maternal uncle badly needed some financial support, which Aakash unfortunately could not help with. Aakash had hardly any savings. He had kept some money aside for his wife's delivery expenses. Aakash was very embarrassed and disappointed as he could not help his dearest one when it was needed.

Aakash used to spend long hours in the office usually. Camellia used to wait for him till late at night. Sometimes, we are forced to follow the life without a choice. Today, Aakash feels bad when he looks back and thinks he could have done a much better job as a husband during that crucial time. It was his fortune that Camellia had never complained about this. Most probably, life had taught her to be patient.

When you carry on with the flow in your early career;

you aspire to buy an apartment, car or some additional household items. Life was going on smoothly between the office and home. In between, Aakash used to go to his native place. Sometimes, his parents used to come to his rented apartment in Kolkata. Then came the day when Aakash got the news that his maternal uncle had died in an accident in the factory. This came as a big blow to Aakash and Camellia. Suddenly, their biggest well-wisher left them alone without any notice. Life is so unpredictable. You never know what is waiting for tomorrow. Your dearest ones are like this. When they leave, they don't even let you guess!

Life continued with its flow. One day, Aakash got a call from home while he was at the office. His landlord's son told him that Camellia was not feeling well. It was 15th August. Aakash came to the hospital in a hurry and the doctor told him that he was not getting the pulse of the kid. When we have the feeling of losing our dearest ones, the experience is unexplainable. The pain is so deep, you cannot even cry out loud. After putting Camellia on emergency, doctor assured that the pulse was back again. Aakash got a relief; life came back again; nothing was lost! The doctor gave the date of delivery and it was August 30th. The countdown began again.

Then, the day came when Aakash and Camellia got their son Rayaan. It's just once in a lifetime that a father prays for his son to cry! A new chapter had opened in Aakash's life. His life was always surrounded by parents, relatives, siblings, friends and Camellia. Now someone else came in, who would take some percentage of his mind and life's share.

Finally You Settle Down Through Hard Work...

Life teaches us everything as the time comes. Gradually, Rayaan started crawling and then standing, too. And, finally the moment came when Rayaan could walk. Rayaan was very cute at this stage. Even the most serious and reserved personality would smile seeing him. Meanwhile, Aakash went to USA for 3 months for his job. It was like a dream come true. He always wanted to see this country. When he finally landed in USA, he could not believe that he had reached his dreamland. These three months, Aakash noticed that climate, people and life were very different there. Infrastructure was made for everyone. People had enough patience to let others cross the road safely. None rushed to move past and ahead of others. Every job had its respect. Every person had freedom.

It was very different from his loving India! After the assignment was over, he came back to India with a few packs of chocolates and gifts for his friends and everyone in the family. His friends and family members wanted to see the pictures he had taken there. They all were stuck with the beauty of the country. Aakash had fun in answering all their questions. In 3 months, Rayaan had grown up as well. At this stage, kids' looks change a lot at a faster pace. In the weekend, Aakash and his family used to travel to his native place. Sometimes, they used to travel in public transport and sometimes, they used to rent a car. At times, Aakash's parents used to come with them to Kolkata. With a new car, they got a driver, Soham who used to stay at a nearby place and was a very decent person.

Life kept on moving in its full swing. At office, it was a busy schedule and at home, it was all about Camellia and Rayaan. But when GOD makes you busy with something, the other part of your life gets less attention. Friends also got busy with their day to day life. The number of connections gradually died down. You don't feel so sad anymore if you don't meet each other often. One day, Aakash got the possession of his newly bought apartment. Aakash and Camellia started preparing to move to the new apartment. Last one year had been very eventful. While Aakash got distant from his friends, he got his best gift in life through Rayaan.

It was another day in the month of June. Aakash woke up in the morning a bit late, in no hurry to go to office. As usual, he started going through the newspaper while having tea with Camellia. He noticed a big news article about a very common ordinary man. This gentleman stayed in a remote village where there was an acute scarcity of water. While the government and administration could not find a solution, this gentleman almost single-handedly dug a pond for the villagers. His effort did not go in vain and the whole village was now getting the needed water in their day to day life. Aakash was completely mesmerized to read the story. This man was a very ordinary person like many of us. But the sincere effort that he had put in, was truly heroic. It does not matter, whether this person was educated or not, rich or poor, rustic or urban. Many people on this planet may not even know him. Aakash saluted this real hero, a living example in leading from the front.

After an hour, Aakash and Camellia went to Rayaan's school. Rayaan and his classmates had planned to have a food festival at the school. Whatever profit they would make, would go to some NGO for social work. Aakash and Camellia went to the food court on time. They went to all possible counters, tasted the food and spoke to many students. Aakash was thrilled to see how Rayaan and his classmates were putting their best efforts to sell food and take the money for a noble cause. Aakash was very impressed with their professionalism and level of energy to make a difference. They came back home with a very happy mind.

In the evening, there was a reality show on television. One person came to a dance show, who was in his late 30's. His mother was in a wheelchair and had come outside her home after seven long years, just to see her son performing. This person had lost his father sometime back. His parents used to dream that their little son would be a good dancer one day. And this man made it on the stage even after 30's! It was a very emotional moment for the man and his mother. Nothing stopped this man to put efforts to make his dream come true.

In the same dance show, another person performed with just one leg. He had lost his leg in an accident four years back. With one leg, his dance was extremely passionate. Everyone applauded his performance. This was great to see such inspiring people around. Age and disability came as odds in their lives. But they never stopped trying. Aakash saluted them all from the bottom of his heart!

Let's connect back to Aakash in his late 20's. They had moved to a new apartment. Now Aakash had a car, apartment, and a good job. Little Rayaan looked more glittering than ever. In the first few months, they became busy in decorating the apartment. They arranged the basic stuff for a family to live decently. Time was running much faster.

Three years back, Aakash had got the break of joining a big information technology company. The US-based company was on a growth trajectory and everyone was in the mood to give their best to take the company to the next level. Working in a team environment brought in a rich experience. This was when his experience in mining company helped him a lot. Soon he discovered himself in a good and winning team. They learnt a lot, worked hard. The information technology industry is a knowledge industry.

The life in this industry is always packed up with thoughts, plans, execution, risks, challenges and how one responds to the challenges. Communication is of utmost importance. It is important to strike a balance between office and life. Otherwise, one may not even realize when a hundred percent of brain memory is occupied with just work!

Aakash was at his best in office. Not only he developed himself as a professional, but he also ensured their team was bonded, trained to handle any situation. Aakash used to believe; however, the pressure he was under, however helpless he was, he would never do anything that pulls down someone.

Aakash has always been a believer of 'humanity first'. We keep on changing organizations. We get into new projects for new clients, our team changes. But what always remains important is, how you are as a human being. The quality time we spend with people is what people remember, even long after you are no more part of the organization. It is fine to sacrifice a short-term accomplishment if it is at the cost of others' inconvenience. Can we ever consider ourselves successful, leaving others behind? Advice from great Nelson Mandela reminds us, "The first thing is to be honest with yourself. You can never have an impact on society if you have not changed yourself..."

When You Are At The Peak...

It was the year 2005. Rayaan was 2 years old then. This October, he went to Denver in Colorado. It was snowing everywhere, and the city used to look scintillating with the backdrop of the rocky mountains. In this client's place, Aakash had some free time. He and his friends made complete use of their time there. He fell in love with the Rocky Mountains. Everything seemed to be like a dream. Then one day, he received a call from Camellia and got to know that his father was not well. Aakash rushed back home in India. The memory of Denver was left behind. Coming back home, they watched the recorded video of Denver. His father was so happy to see the country. Next day, they went to shop together. His father was walking very slowly. Aakash thought his father's weak eyesight had caused this slow gait. When they came back home, they planned that they would go to their hometown for *Saraswati Puja*. Next day, Aakash took his father to the hospital for a checkup. Doctor advised his father to get admitted in the hospital for a few days as his health was not well. His father did not listen to the doctor's advice. He said "I am absolutely fine. I don't need to get admitted to a hospital." Aakash and his father had a debate on this decision and finally, his father won.

Next day, Aakash woke up when Camellia called him at very early morning. His father was on the floor and he had collapsed when he had tried to go to the rest room. His father was in a terribly bad shape. Aakash did not even know how much time he had been in that state. They took him to the doctor's place. A few kilometers seemed to be light years to reach the hospital. Everything had finished in just an hour's time. His father did not even give him time to take care. When you see your father bidding you by in an hour's time, you can't express that heartbreaking feeling. Losing father is like the biggest shock in one's life. The person, who had helped Aakash dream so much, was no more to share his rest of the journey. What happened next for two days was something Aakash does not even want to remember. It was as if you took a long time to paint a few pictures and you have been asked to erase them now one by one.

Aakash and his family, siblings, relatives; all went to their village home. His mother was alone. They all spent two weeks together. Everyone was there except his father! Maybe, even after death, he had brought every- one together back to their old home. A lot of old people and well-wishers came to their home to pay homage to his father. His father's old friends and school colleagues also came to see him for the last time. Aakash got to know more about his father from them. His father was not rich, nor was he an eminent person. With his limited capacity, whatever he had achieved, Aakash was proud of his father. When someone finally departs this world, he or she is remembered for his or her work. Every good work is recognized at some or the other point in time. Aakash knew well that his father would be remembered for long even after he had passed away.

Life never leaves us behind. We need to walk together and move on. Whatever romanticism he Aakash brought from Denver, went under the cover post his father's sudden death. Aakash and his family came back to Kolkata. His mother wanted to stay back in their village home. Aakash felt to let his mother stay back some more time to settle down. During a difficult situation, we may not always know what is good and what is not. It took some time to adjust and life again started its journey back on track. Rayaan also had come to the age of three years by then. In a nuclear family, kids don't get time to mingle with others. Parents get very busy with their own work and activities. Therefore, the kind of places like playschools are like blessings for the kids. They get to meet other kids, teachers, and many others. They get to play a lot. This gives them the needed confidence to grow up. Very soon, Rayaan developed basic skills. One important lesson that Aakash would always carry is supporting a kid during early education. We all need to support our kids to grow up. Kids can learn very fast. They can unlearn and learn anything through guided support. The playschool helped Rayaan secure his admission to a primary school. He was really enjoying his time in the playschool. By now, Aakash had reached his early 30's. He had a decent job. In his career, he was doing extremely well. His dream to see the USA had been met. His family had also settled by now. This was the time, Aakash wanted to set up a playschool. He and one of his friends started the school. Their relentless effort made the school popular in no time. Every weekend, Aakash used to go to a nearby railway station to put their advertisement leaflets inside the newspapers. They went on putting the advertisement banners at key locations in the locality. They utilized every parent-teacher meeting to emphasize on the need for child education. Above all, through this school, Aakash and his friend could provide jobs to ten people. In parallel, during the weekdays, they continued with their jobs. Aakash got an enriching experience in childhood education.

Sometimes certain events change our direction and focus. This happened to Aakash as well. Suddenly, the situation in his office changed. He was told to take a long-term assignment in USA. His business partner gave him an assurance that he would take care of the school. Aakash finally decided to go to USA. This time, Camellia and Rayaan accompanied him. His mother and close friends came to send him off at the airport. It was an emotional moment when you move forward to an unknown world, leaving behind a big world of the known.

Great Things Inspire Us...

Three of them reached New Jersey in the month of February. For Camellia and Rayaan, this was the first international trip. The night they had landed, it was snowing. They got into a hotel and took a studio type room. Aakash had some other colleagues in the same hotel. He made all the initial formalities in first couple of weeks. They stayed for almost two months in the hotel. Aakash still remembers the smell of the carpet in the hotel. For the first time, Camellia and Rayaan had experienced the snowfall. Staying in hotel is a different experience, altogether. You get all the benefits and limit your life to service offerings. In the weekend, they used to go to the supermarket, meet friends and colleagues. Weekend was always a party time!

After two months, they moved to a rented an apartment in nearby residential community. It used to take hardly 10 minutes for him to reach office. Aakash used to come to home during the lunch. There was lot of work, but it was manageable. Working hard during the weekdays and partying even harder in the weekend had become a regular routine. Aakash used to wonder how this country was made so clean, beautiful and disciplined. The infrastructure was flawless. They did not differentiate between a city and a remote place. Everyone had the basic rights and facilities, irrespective of where they stayed. The roads were just great. People followed the traffic rules. Police was very strict, and everyone was cautious of the rules. Aakash and his family used to go to a nearby park. There were hardly a few people around. That park was like their own private place. They had a nearby library, as well. During the off-time, they used to bring books and video cassettes from this library. This was another place, where the friends used to meet each other.

After couple of months, Aakash admitted Rayaan in a nearby public school. On the first day, it was a very strange experience for both, Rayaan and his parents. Rayaan was just 5 years old then and was a bit nervous on his first day to school. When Aakash took him to school, he started crying. An aged lady teacher came forward and told Aakash, "Don't worry. He will be alright. I promise you, when you meet him at end of the day, his face will have all the smiles in the world". The lady teacher was Mrs. Lightner. Aakash left the school with a lot of anxiety. In the afternoon, he came from office to Rayaan's school to pick him up. All the students were coming out from their classes. From a distance, Aakash could see Rayaan coming out, holding Mrs. Lightner's hand. His face was bright, with lots of happiness and joy. Mrs. Lightner was indeed right!

Whenever Aakash had some time, he used to go to Rayaan's school. He loved to meet the teachers and participate in social events. He noticed that students were taught to do things the right way. Students were encouraged to try things through practical experience. Be it, the bus service, or a school event; everywhere, there was a process in place. Teachers were very passionate about their teaching jobs. They used to care a lot for the kids. In the parent-teacher meetings, they used to encourage both, student and the parents. Students were very proud of their country. They learnt to keep the surroundings clean. They were taught to respect fellow people. Every kid was made aware of security and safety mechanisms and the process to seek help. Kids were never put under unnecessary pressure. They were encouraged to do what they enjoyed most. There was no rat race, no bad feelings. Maybe, that's why this country produced ample number of great people on the planet.

In office, Aakash noticed they heavily banked on

expertise, process, technology and tools. People were very time conscious. Meetings used to start and end at the right time, respecting people's time. Employees believed in quality, rather than just quantity. Escalation was there to seek help, not to put someone under unnecessary radar. Aakash met some of the fantastic technology leaders in this company. He was simply impressed with their knowledge, quality focus and leadership skills. This was where Aakash had got his second professional guru. He was a born leader with great management skills. His working style empowered his team. His support during the crisis time made him a natural leader. He knew how to defend his team, and how to extract most from every available talent. If you ever get an opportunity to work with such a person, you only get to learn great stuff. At office, Aakash was playing a very responsible role. At home, he could give his best for the family. In his friend circle, he was always willing to foster a long-lasting bond.

When your surroundings are great, you can only think of adding your part to that greatness. At the most basic level, it is the people who make the society, a country. Every place Aakash roamed in US, he was overwhelmed with the unparallel infrastructure and cleanliness of the surroundings. There was not much difference in terms of basic services across rural life and that of urban. People had patience to let others go first. People had energy to say 'Hello' to everyone, even if it was to a stranger. Basic education is always important to live a humane life. That keeps people hungry for knowledge, energetic to participate and contribute, and eager to stay social. If any country is ahead of others, it is because of its leaders and more importantly, because of the people. Discipline makes the foundation of such societies and nations stronger. This is something deeply planted in the very childhood, through families, schools and societies.

Change Is The Only Constant...

Life brings lot of surprises and mind's trajectory is also hard to predict. While everything was going great for Aakash, of late his health was not supporting him. Moreover, while he appreciates USA as a country, he had always India, family and friends, there in his mind. Camellia also wanted to go back to India, as she also missed India to a large extent. The only aspect they were a bit stuck was about Rayaan's education. It was not an easy decision to take the family back to India when Rayaan had completely settled in US. Finally, they made their minds to come back. It was a very emotional moment. In one hand, they were eager to go back. On the other hand, they knew they would miss the country, people and freedom.

Last few weeks in US was all about seeing few places for the last time. His friends and colleagues in US were very upset. When Aakash looks back, he understands that he never wanted to settle down anywhere, by just being another person. Had he stayed back there, most probably, he could have afforded much better standards of living. However, Aakash always wanted to do something for his society, back in India. He never had set a too rigid target for his success in terms of just few materialistic gains. The meaning of success in his mind was deeply rooted during his childhood itself. And that was 'Do something for the people, be the change in their living, bring the smile on their faces. Does not matter at what scale you end up achieving them.' It was time to pack up, go back home and do something for what he had dreamt all through his life.

It was December 2009 when Aakash and family came

back to India. The Winter in India did not make them miss the climate of US. Initial few days, they worked hard to bring home back on rolling. Rayaan was again readmitted to his previous school. It took some days to settle down in office and meet many more new faces. Aakash and family used to spend the weekends in their native place.

Meanwhile, Aakash noticed that something had been missing, though everything seemed to be in place just as before. Of course, everyone was much worried about their lives and livelihoods; earning money, getting married, building a small home, there was indeed a lot to think of. Many in his known circle was going through a struggling phase. When one goes through a rough phase in life, one tends to forget smiling, hide from others, and not to share the joys and sorrows of life. Aakash understood this, but he did not have a long-term solution for these problems. At times, he used to financially help some of his closed ones. How much that little money would help? There was no long-term solution to their miseries.

This was the time, Aakash thought that appropriate time had come to contribute to the society. With a lot of encouragement from Camellia, Aakash founded a society, named 'Yatra' with couple of other friends. The objective was to encourage rural youth to set up a 'Yatra' center, where children would be learning something that regular school did not focus on much, in rural areas. Children would learn basic computer science. They would learn how to communicate in English. They would be trained in dance, art and Craft. At the same time, the owner of the center would earn some money through minimal tuition fees. Some youngsters would get job as faculties and center administrators.

Aakash was confident that this would help the villages to a large extent, in preparing the next generation well. Aakash and his couple of friends explored around their village and surrounding areas. Finally, they could open their first school in their own village. They talked to multiple people, parents, and students. They recruited the faculties and trained the faculties to work in accordance with the principle and objective of the society. Over a period, many students joined the school. They used to have parent-teacher meetings. Art and craft and dance competitions were held to create the interest in students' minds. Aakash had lots of pleasure through true accomplishment in his own village.

Every weekend, Aakash used to come to this center from Kolkata. He used to spend couple of hours with the children. His intention was to understand those kids better and motivate them to try and perform better. He was very happy to see the glittering faces of those rural children. There were discussions with the parents to explain them why it was important to learn certain things during the early stage of child education. Sometimes, he felt it very difficult to get the right kind of administrators and faculties for the center. He hoped that one day some of these students would grow up and take bigger responsibilities to take the center forward. While the center was doing well, Aakash understood managing and raising the center to his level of expectation required more of his time. Remotely, it was difficult to ensure the kind of ambience, he was thinking of. He continued to try his best with multiple odds on its way.

There are certain phases in life, when despite you giving your best efforts, you may not meet your own expectations. Moreover, there are many external factors that impact and influence your path in the journey. By then lot of efforts given; lot of money spent for this 'yatra' center. There was no dearth of courage and planning. Still, things were not going in the right direction. Aakash was not at his best from personal side. There were many changes in the office circle. Aakash understood that things were happening beyond his control and many times, he was just at the receiving end.

Aakash knew that he could not compromise with certain core values. To him, it was always important to with integrity and self-respect. He loves to be remembered more as a human being than everything else.

Very soon, he understood it was high time to bid goodbye to his then-current organization and move on. It was not an easy decision. When you stay in a place for almost a decade, it is no more just a workplace. You create your own network, friendship and support system. Then, the day came when he really called for a day to move on. Aakash understood it was fine to move to a new place and try afresh. Change is the only constant in life. Last couple of months just went by like a whiff of air. During his last few weeks, his not so close colleagues came closer and the closer ones started to maintain a distance. The knowns became more unknown and the unknowns renewed their friendships. Life is full of learning. Every turn leaves certain things behind and unfolds a new part of it.

Stay Lifelong Student To Embrace The New...

It was middle of the year 2011. Aakash had many bindings in Kolkata; his apartment, car, land, son's school, family, friends and closed ones. On top of everything, he had 'Yatra' in his village. He was thirty-six years old then. Everything in Kolkata was well settled. He opted to resign from his office and move on. He had some hope that he would get some opportunity in Kolkata itself. But to his surprise, nothing worked out and he did not have any option other than relocating to a new city.

After a lot of consideration, he decided to go alone and Camellia and Rayaan would stay back in Kolkata. He hoped he would come back in a while. Then a day came, he left for the new city and workplace. The journey to this phase was full of unknowns, leaving behind all his comfort back in Kolkata. Life changed all of a sudden. He came to Bangalore, stayed in a single room rented place. He understood he needed to commute via bus as he had kept the car back in Kolkata. Joining office, he realized he no longer had a personal cabin. He was asked to sit anywhere on the bench and everyday someone or the other was taking his place and he had to look for a new one. He was very new to this place and office. Hardly a couple of folks knew him. He understood he must wait and watch before he got into some real work to establish himself.

One day, to his surprise, he met an old friend. Aakash had helped him in his last organization as a supervisor. When this gentleman was going through a professional crisis, Aakash had stood by him unconditionally. After the initial chat, his friend understood Aakash was a 'nobody' here, given he had just started in this place. His friend could not match this new version of Aakash to what he had seen him as before. He almost forced Aakash to meet one of the senior leaders in the organization. And that meeting helped him secure a critical role in Hyderabad. Soon he moved to Hyderabad and literally fell in love with the city on his first visit; the city, infrastructure, climate, people – everything was just amazing!

It was all about work on weekdays and exploring here and there in the city on the weekends. Aakash learnt to manage things at home on his own. He became much more self-sufficient. He made many new friends in the city. Every month, he used to go to Kolkata and every alternate month, his mother, Camellia and son used to visit Hyderabad. Like that, twenty months passed by. This was a great experience of learning to embrace change in life when you have lost touch of many old good things.

Aakash was very happy to have his wife and son moved to Hyderabad permanently after twenty long months. First couple of months passed by, for setting up the home front. At office, his career experienced a complete positive swing with promotion, and good ratings. Aakash applied all his professional learnings in new place. Whatever he was assigned to, he was passionate about executing it in perfect style. He earned confidence from colleagues, seniors, and clients. Opportunities started flowing in. Rayaan started finding his school great. He was encouraged a lot to try more, very similar in line with his experience in USA. Camellia also got settled into the vibe of the new city. She made a good number of friends around. Aakash was very happy to see his family so well adjusted in the new place.

The change brought in renewed energy in Aakash and his family, as if they had just started living again. Positive vibes moved them forward in their journeys. Obstacles seemed natural ways to move on for betterment. They were doing what they liked the most. They travelled to many places around. They had get-togethers with many friends. Rayaan participated in all possible events in his school. It was like a dream run. Every six months, they used to go to Kolkata and their native village. At times they missed Kolkata and people there. However, the new city gave them many new as well. A renewed network gave them new meaning to their lives. Life moves on. While we miss the past, new things always keep you on toes to move on. It depends on how we embrace the 'new' and stay positive to live life. God balances us and gives us internal strength to find new purpose in lives. We just need to stay lifelong students!

You Are Reminded For Giving Back...

This August, Aakash to the age of 45. It had been a long journey from a small village to the corporate world. The journey till this stage was not always easy. He spent great and worst moments with mixed feelings. In a span of few years, he had lost his maternal uncle, father, and grandmother. Many closed ones became distant. Many new faces came closer. Rayaan came in his life with a renewed purpose. Aakash made new friends and colleagues. On professional side, he had reached many milestones. Even though, he never seriously focused on money too much, he ended up buying properties, and a luxury car. Financially, he was not rich, but got a good enough balance to lead a life decently. On personal side, Camellia was now well trained in art and craft. Besides managing her home, she became very passionate about it. In 18 years of marriage, this was one thing Camellia had been very serious about. Rayaan was doing well in his education. He was enjoying the freedom to choose what he wanted to study. What else Aakash could expect from life?

A person like Aakash never stops dreaming. No accomplishment makes him feel complacent. It is his mind that raises the bar always higher. When Aakash travels in the flight, he sees the earth below through the white clouds. Even the big structures on this planet, look very small from that height. In this universe, nothing is absolutely big. Rather the biggest of things are just like dots in the sphere. We look at things relative to our own scale only. It all depends on at what scale we view and assess what appears in front of us.

We can only enlarge our scale to some extent through our journey, experience, learning and action. Successful people do that diligently and with unmatched commitment. More than professional success, Aakash had set a higher yardstick for himself as a human being. He always dreamt of a place where everyone would be treated equally. He has been a strong believer in love and respect. His philosophy towards life always revolved around helping others achieve greater success. Is that enough? Does Aakash think today that he could do all that he wanted to do? The reality is different. Human thinks it can do a lot. However, in the larger sphere of the universe, nothing is as big as it appears to us. More importantly, nothing stays here forever. The strongest and the ablest person on earth can bring in only a slight change on this planet.

Most of the human beings lead a well-guided life. They get trained, experienced, live their lives, do their best and one day, they retire forever. There are few exceptions; who are passionate about something, go that extra mile, stay very committed and focused on their goals, and don't leave till they achieve it. They are the likes of Sachin Tendulkar, Maradona, Barack Obama, Steve Jobs and Bill Gates. Their commitment is unparallel. Their personal sacrifices to reach their goal are unmatched. Their love and passion for something grows day by day, irrespective of any initial accomplishments or challenges. They are most probably few of those who can tell themselves, "Yes, I am what I wanted to be". What happens to rest of the people like Aakash? Don't they try enough? Don't they have enough commitment? Are they mentally not determined enough to stay focused on what they wanted to achieve?

In fact, many ordinary people have achieved a lot in their lives. Some of them have brilliant stories around how they had reached that level through a very hostile path. They are the heroes to some parents, siblings, children, spouse, friends, colleagues, and society. It is just that their scale may not be as large as that of extremely successful people, known globally. But that does not make their accomplishments any less. They also have great stories. It is just that their reader base is not that wide. In his childhood, Aakash used to dream in those dark nights. Hot summers used to add energy in his minds. During rain, drops of water used to touch his bodies to wake him up. There were people around him, ready to support in the most difficult time. When you are in a lagging team, and your teammates encourage you to move on, that's the greatest support one can have in life. Others wish and dream for you more than what you can, for yourself. Think of those parents who sacrificed everything, just to see their kids happy. Think of that grandmother who being herself, uneducated, relentlessly encouraged her grandchildren to study and be successful in life. Think of those childhood friends, who never achieved anything in lives, but still took so much pride just because you had achieved more. Think of that old teacher, who used to come to a school on bicycles from a distant village and still could create long-lasting interest in students' minds?

Seeing these people around, when you grow up, can you think of just yourself? Your past reminds you, "It's your turn. Do something for the people, for the society. Give them back." This is the reason, Aakash could not accept living just a comfortable life. Success in his view has never been just moving up the corporate ladder. It is rather a career milestone. His intent has always been to touch the lives of people in whatever small way he could. Nothing ever got a higher priority in his life than staying human. He is one of those people who believe, it is okay to retire as a mid-level executive, but not at all okay to finish this life without much contribution to society. He is ready to take a bit lower rating in professional life, but he can't accept anything below average in his personal, human life.

Long Race? Time To Take A Pause...

Aakash did not go to office today. It's raining heavily. He is sitting in his balcony, in a rest chair. Through the fog, his eyes are trying to reach as far as possible. The tall housing towers barricade on his way of vision. In last 45 years, he had got to learn a lot in life, both on personal and professional sides. With time, many things became distant, many new things came in his life as strangers. All through this journey, what had remained constant was his aspiration to help people. During his childhood, they used to play cricket amongst the locals. There used to be a match between the neighbors. They did not have a wooden bat or a wicket. They used to make their bats and wickets using bamboo. He played cricket with at least hundreds of his local friends. Even now, when they meet each other, they talk about those old golden days.

Aakash remembers how they used to collect money, cook food and serve them in their surrounding flood ridden areas. It was a great sense of accomplishment with every plate of food served to the kids and old people. Aakash can't believe now that they made this possible when they were just teens, with just some friends, not even educated or financially well off. We can achieve anything and everything through positive vibes and the right intent. When Aakash was in his childhood, they used to see that others who were a bit well off, used to celebrate *Holi* (festival of colors). He and his friends also started celebrating *Holi* in their society. This was the day, every family in the society used to celebrate with colors and in the evening, they used to have dinner together. At least for a day, people used to have dinner together and every kid and every adult used to have a lot of fun during the evening program. There was hardly any well-established family in that society. But with the pride and pleasure of togetherness, they used to come together for a day in the year.

Aakash's village was very famous for the *Laxmi Puja* celebration. Aakash and his friends knew that it was not possible to celebrate in a grand way due to the financial state of their society members. They started *Laxmi Puja* in their society with everyone contributing their best. This was the time, Aakash and his classmates started organizing a movie theater and through the profit, they contributed for a library in the village. These days, Aakash can't attend these festivals with his friends that often. But those festivals become so successful events now, that even the new generation is organizing these festive events with lots of energy and enthusiasm.

There were many such accomplishments, and they had achieved them during the early stage of their lives, when getting a full egg in lunch was like having a luxury meal. All these memories tell Aakash that to do something good and impactful, money is not the only vehicle. One must be very committed, must instill a positive hope and dream in people's minds to achieve larger social impacts. In India, there are many challenges – lack of quality education, unemployment, pollution, poverty and many more. if someone really wants to start something good and impactful for society, many Aakash would come forward. This country knows how to work for people, even if that calls for sacrificing personal aspirations.

Being a salaried employee, Aakash continued helping his friends with whatever he could. But his money was not enough for helping others, over a long time. He had set up a school, leased a hotel, and nothing worked for his friends.

He had started 'Yatra', but over the time, that also did not create enough opportunities for his friends. Sometimes his disappointments grew. But the very next day, he used to come back with a positive mind to do something new again. Whatever failure he had faced, his learning experience enriched.

Aakash left us one day for bringing changes in his own society. Is he on the right path? Did he try enough for his closed ones? Is he satisfied inside his mind for whatever he did with limited ability? Did Aakash achieve all that he had dreamt one day? The question comes in mind, again and again, "Am I what I wanted to be?" Aakash thinks through all of this and believes that he did many things, but the journey is yet not over. He needs to do more and can't stop with just what he has done so far.

We all wanted to be someone someday. Very few people know the secret of staying focused on their goals. Few reach their destination. Most of us try hard to fit in the reality and end up being something else. Our lives are short-lived. Many of us may not even realize that with passage of every moment, we are nearing closer to the finishing line. One day, we just say goodbye with empty hands, just like the way we came into this world. Steve Jobs, co-founder of Apple Inc., a pioneer of the personal computer era confessed, "My favorite things in life don't cost any money. It's really clear that the most precious resource we all have is time."

Between life and death what remains is a journey. In this bigger world, any human being, however successful he or she is, cannot bring all the changes that we dream for. However, we must try our best to contribute our part. It does not matter if we are not 'Sachin Tendulkar' or a 'Barack Obama'. In our own circle and surroundings, we can set examples in some ways. We, the common people can also have a similar sense of accomplishment as much as that Sachin gets after reaching a world record. Only difference is the scale and reach, though our heroics may be the same.

We all have the aspiration to be someone. Through our actions we must believe, we are what we want to be. It's our life and we can shape it up!

With Age Comes Clarity...

We all may not be able to bring a big change on this planet. But we can do smaller things with passion. We can start that journey at home with our family members. At workplace, we can impact the lives of many of our colleagues. We can make many more friends in our society. We must utilize every opportunity to do our own part. At his mid-forty, Aakash realized that life is not just thinking of doing something. The world would not change overnight just like that. It is rather all about doing things your- self with passion. We will see how common men like Aakash, and many others could do small things in great way. When one starts a good initiative, it spreads and creates interest in others' minds. A few more join hands. Together, they add to a significant impact on our society. That's the way to go for a common man!

Staying connected with the friends and near ones is very important in our life. We are nothing without our dear ones. In a global world, we all are distant through geo-coordinates. We can't meet our nearest ones as frequently as we used to do. Everyone is very busy nowadays. During his childhood, Aakash sometimes used to connect his friends through letters. He could not meet his friends almost a year. After long time, Aakash started writing to his friends again.

My friends,

After a long time, I am writing to you. I trust, however distant we are today; you would read this letter at least once. I recall, together we spent many days, months and years. We started walking our dreams together in the childhood. We had our own share of fun, even during the difficult – most time in our lives. Since then, our roads may have turned to different directions. At times, we crossed each other. Sometimes, we exchanged smiles. Many times, we couldn't even stop and talk with our hearts. We all are busy with our very own journeys. But I know if something goes wrong, we still have enough reasons to jump in for helping each other.

I know we don't play anymore in that ground. The pond beside our school does not experience our relentless swimming and arising waves. Our mothers don't come and show us big eyes to order us to leave the pond. We don't go to the movie hall together anymore. Not sure, if those bicycles are still functioning or not, which we used to ride to the nearby places. We don't go to that 100 Feet road for gathering in the afternoon. We don't need to worry about taking 3 rupees from our father's wallet for buying cigarettes. Maybe our succeeding generation nowadays go for picnics on 25th December. During Holi, we don't need to estimate the expense budget anymore. We don't need to stay awake till late at night for the Puja Pandal. Many things, we don't need to do anymore.

We don't need them. We are not staying together anymore. For just a couple of days in a year, we happen to meet each other. I know some of you may even think, what's the point in meeting? We are no more in the same boat. That's natural. I don't blame anyone for that.

You may think some of us have been more successful and living a decent life. You may think you don't have time for rest of your friends. Yes, some of us may be a bit well off in terms of job and position. Maybe some are a little bit more tied up than the others. Some of us are struggling and getting frustrated with what life offers them. We all try to help each other with whatever little we possess. I realize that is not enough to pull up one from that deep hole. It pains me as much as you suffer. You know why?

Because we dreamt together. Because you were with me all through those days when I was not whoever I am today. You don't know how much you encouraged me to move on and achieve greater success. I can't forget your unconditional support in every sphere of life. My success in examination used to bring smiles on your faces. When I cracked the engineering entrance examination, you were proud more than me. You wanted to see me move ahead always. Friends, how do I forget those days?

However distant I am today; my mind and heart are always with you. Last 25 years, we may not be staying closer to each other. But there has never been a single day when our childhood faces did not mirror in my mind. We most probably could not financially lift the few of us. Still, I am happy to see that even in the rough phase of life; you still are so honest and sincere. I know you might be sleeping with an empty stomach, but you won't steal a single rupee from anyone. I know however tired you are, you won't mind helping that old poor man on the roadside.

I am proud that even with so many odds in life, you have still maintained your humanity. What more we could expect? My request to each one of you is that you must not leave hope in your life. Never stop dreaming. Each one of you is a hero to your parents, wives and children. All of you are very honest, and if you put your best efforts, I am sure you would sleep with a smile. If I can achieve some professional goal, some other friends can achieve their aspirations, you all can meet your dream. This December, we all are going to meet again in person. I am sure we will go back to our childhood for few days. Let's walk, sing and smile together. Why don't we play another football match in that old ground?

I am attaching train tickets and hotel bookings for us all to go and meet in Darjeeling. You must have remembered that we used to plan our Darjeeling tour before. I am so excited about this trip. Let's forget all our downsides for few days and bring back some golden time together.

What made me write this letter today? I know life is too short. Don't know, if I will get another chance to tell you this tomorrow. I am writing a book. You all are there in my story; my heroes. Pray like you always did before. There are so many 'Aakash' now chasing their dream, dream to change the way we think; a dream to see a balanced world without any difference; a dream to make this planet a better one. If some of these people read this book, I can tell myself finally, "See! I am what I want to be!"

I hope, through this book, I would be able to contribute in the society more than what I could through my little job. I am writing this book for you all. It's midnight and I would go to bed. I know you all must be sleeping by now. Sleep tight and stay happy, my friends. Stay human, as always!

Will not say Bye

See you soon. Your friend, Aakash!

Few months passed by. It was 30th August, and Aakash was still in office in the evening. He knew it was Rayaan's birthday. He had promised to give him something special this time. Aakash knew the book was not complete yet. He would like to take a print and gift this incomplete story to his son. Aakash did not know even that his new journey would start with this story. And it was all about doing small things, doing with passion. Aakash wanted to complete this story since the last 3 months. He succeeded to finish only one fourth of it. Because he had started, he was able to gift story to Rayaan. It is important to stay focused on what we want to achieve. There may be distractions, but we must keep on trying.

Aakash wrote on the cover page, "Happy birthday, my son! I am sure you will love this small gift. I promise to complete this in 2020 and you will get the complete version then." He came back home that night with a cake to celebrate Rayaan's birthday. He handed over the incomplete story to Rayaan. Together, they spent some time and finally, Rayaan went to his bedroom with the new gift. He read the story for an hour, glanced through the pages and was amazingly happy and hugged his father. Aakash could feel the happiness on Rayaan's face. There are moments that you can't buy through costly gifts. There are certain things that need a personal touch and those caring touches impact our lives to a large extent.

Whatever happened tonight, made Aakash rethink on his philosophy towards life. We dream to achieve greater success in our journeys. At times, we may feel exhausted or distracted due to many surprises in life. At the end of the day, what remains is how much we tried, how much we could do and how much appetite we still must have to do even more. We all need to live in the present and aspire to achieve with what we have and who we are. We must try doing small things in great way. That makes even a very ordinary person to accomplish greater heights in life.

Think What You Want To Do...

If we see our lives, they always have a 'me' at the center. And it is surrounded by our family, closed ones, friends, colleagues and neighbors. Together they form the virtual society we live in. Many smaller societies, in turn, form the nation. Every nation is ultimately a factor of 'me' and 'us' only. We don't realize always, how impactful we all can be in the making of our nation. Most of the common people like Aakash remain very busy with 'me' and 'family'. The hard life loves them so much that they can't get out of that close love-net. Even being confined, we all have immense power to shape the place we live in, to a better place for ourselves!

It was mid-October. Aakash had gone for local sightseeing with a couple of his friends and families. The place was surrounded by green all over. Silence seemed to be the answer to all questions one might have. Beauty of nature asked them to relax and behold. The guest house was surrounded by forest and dam. It was a great reunion of fresh air and clean water in presence of dense forest and deep silence. Late in the evening, Aakash was sitting in the balcony. The dam nearby was no more visible amid darkness all around. If you had seen the surroundings during the daytime, it was easy to imagine the place. However, you can't afford to see it again till the morning breaks the night. Aakash's inner mind was also going through a similar strange feeling. Through the darkest night, he could imagine his path so far. From his childhood, he had met so many people in different places. Many incidents had only increased his aspiration to achieve more in life. He was already in his mid-forties. His mind did not want to wait anymore. His inner-self told him that night, "Let's break the night and slip into the light of morning. Let's start doing those things that you had always wanted to accomplish."

What did Aakash want to accomplish? Why did not he focus on it? What did hold him back in trying to achieve his aspiration? By then, he understood that neither he had plenty of money that he could use to bring a positive change in people's lives, nor he believed anymore that money was the only means to meet what he had aspired for. All he needed was his own time, focus and commitment to do that, he always wanted to do.

The basic needs of our lives keep us busy. We need a home, need to have a car, need to be financially sound enough to manage our living standards. On top of that, we have plans for our families, and next generation. We want to secure their living as well. And we must work hard, earn money to do this, and that absorbs so much time and energy from us, we are left with no time to think through what really makes us happy.

It is important for us to stay focused on our work. That's what keeps us moving in our lives. We also need to remind ourselves that we do work to live, not live to work. To be truly accomplished, we need to click the right balance in our lives. If that calls for defining a disciplined routine, so be it. Aakash now believes that one who is not taking care of himself, can't do anything for others. We must first take care of ourselves.

It is important to secure our family's unconditional support in our journey. How many times did you feel lonely and helpless in your journey, just because you did not take your family with you? We must spend enough time with our family as they are an integral part of our lives. Can we ever ignore friendship even for a day in our life? To Aakash, success has no meaning in life if friends don't step up in their personal lives. There is a lot to do to bring back smiles on their faces. There is no bigger sense of accomplishment than seeing our family and friends happy.

Life is too short to relax and wait for tomorrow to live our dreams. With time passing by so fast, distance is bound to come between us. In the social networking age, it is even more important to find opportunities to stay closer to each other. And the best way to stay closer to our friends is to hold their hands and walk together. Did not we all do that in our childhoods? All these things put us in the right frame of mind to do something for our own society. Anything that we do for the society has a long-lasting effect on our lives. What we give to society today, only returns to us again tomorrow, and many times even being multiplied.

Aakash has tried many things in the last couple of decades. In some cases, he was successful in achieving what he had dreamt of. However, it was still not done, leveled to his expectations. When Aakash looks back, he realizes it is not just about trying once a while and wait for the outcome. What matters most is the consistent commitment and focus to meet one's aspirations. Nothing happens without our active participation, commitment and involvement. Things start rolling only when you put yourself at the front to drive the initiative the way you dreamt it. None can live your dream. The truth is people start believing in something when they see it in front of them. Aakash realizes that although he had tried his part, most probably there was even a bigger scope for him to really drive them from the front end and include as many people as possible to expand the scale.

Aakash now realizes, it is not about if he is what he wanted to be. There is no existence of such absolute accomplishments or failures in life. It is rather his belief and activities that affirm if he is what he wants to be. In his mid-forties, he is convinced that he will give his best to make those things happen, that he had cherished so long. Aakash follows what the American print and broadcast journalist, Germany Kent wrote, “Hit the reset button. Whatever happened yesterday, forget about it. Get a new perspective. Today is a new day. A fresh start begins now.”

Set Yourself Right...

Whatever we aspire to achieve, there is no better goal than setting oneself right first. How many times you thought to achieve something, and your fitness came on your way as an obstacle? With age and professional hazards, we sometimes lose an edge on the health side. Not so good health leads to restlessness in mind. Every year, we wait for a good hike, recognition, promotion and much more. And we fail to realize that we are losing another year from our lives! We keep on waiting for our kids to grow up and move to college. We think of when our investment would mature to achieve financial stability. What is there to wait for? Is it not just killing our limited time in this journey? Rather do something that happens now, that you enjoy doing. As Brittany Josephina, a writer and an empowerment coach had said, "The most important day is the day you decide you're good enough for yourself. It's the day you set yourself free."

If you have dreams to realize, better stay disciplined, fit and healthy to live that dream. Last December, Aakash went to his village to attend the centenary year celebration of his school. Some of his friends were at the front to drive this event. Aakash provided his suggestions through email, phone calls to do his part. His friends did their best. It was not perfect; however, this was what his friends could do with limited time and effort people could offer for this program. He had passed out from this school 25 years back. The current students were not even born at that time. Most of the current teachers are new faces for Aakash. He was a well known personality during his school days, because of his background, friendly nature and academic results. After 25 years, when he came to the school, very few people recognized him. He no more had that special feeling of being a prominent student. He met few old friends, teachers and staff. Many of his friends looked older than their actual age. Many still maintained their health and appearance. Aakash understood time has taken many things away from life. He has received many awards in his professional life across the globe. He felt that he must try to achieve many more milestones in his personal life that he always had aspired for. The event in his school made him more determined to reach his personal goal; his willingness to stay fit emerged to be even stronger to reach his goal.

Aakash has made a point to exercise at least 30 minutes every day. If we can work for 12 hours, can't we just spend 30 minutes for ourselves? Eating healthy food is another aspect that Aakash has paid attention to. And sleep? He has almost forgotten that a human needs seven hours of good sleep daily. His body and mind badly needed rest and sleep. He discussed this with his family and consciously brought in a discipline in his day to day life. He could hear the 'secret of life'; the magic of positive thinking inviting constructive actions, leading to positive outcomes in our lives.

When we get too much engrossed into something, be that personal and professional, we don't see how we get gradually distant from our nearest ones. Through a little bit of tweak in his day to day life, Aakash could see how his family responded to positive changes. His wife and son are so happy to see a renewed avatar of Aakash. His wife also joined him in many such positive changes. When we bring in changes in our daily routines to align with the art of living, we see the response in our bodies. Our minds get fresh in thinking and doing even more. Even if we can't love everyone, at least we must love ourselves.

Together, we make our family a happy one! On the

psychological side, Aakash wanted to bring in two important changes; the first one being more social. In the last few years, Aakash has been so focused on just family and his profession; he did not ever feel to mingle with unknowns and strangers. He made a new resolution that he would not let go of any single opportunity to connect to people. Be it in office, his housing, anywhere he goes, he must make meaningful connections.

It gives a great pleasure to take a pause, shake hands with others and exchange smiles and share some moments. We have so limited time in our hands. Why waste the opportunity in knowing more people? There may be a day when you will have the willingness to meet people, but you may not have eyes to look at others, you may not be strong enough to walk and go to the next-door person and say "Hello" You may have many things to share, but you may lose your voice over the age. Never miss moments to share with others!

Aakash started reaching out to his old friends and known faces. Wherever he goes, he finds a special interest to meet new people. At times, he stopped going by his own car, rather took the public transport just to find opportunities to meet and connect different people. Try it sometimes and you would be amazed to see so many interesting people on this planet. It would be a great experience to know them from a close distance. There is so much to learn from each other. We are not just remembered for our education, profession or the chair we hold. It is our behavior and the way we treat people is what people remember about us!

Another goal that Aakash had set up for himself was to be fearless and remove all hesitations. It is a crime if we confine our minds and don't allow it to surface up and share our feelings and thoughts. There is no meaning of being afraid and not speaking up in a forum where it is essential to speak up. How many times, have you observed in a workshop that someone else spoke up what was going on in your mind? How many times did you discover that you knew the right answer, but you still did not attempt to? How many times did you want to participate in a program and remained silent and did not raise your hand to come on the stage?

Because of our self-imprisonment, many times we lose the opportunity that knocks on our door. At mid-forty, Aakash no more wants to live like that. He said to himself, "Enough is enough. I must not lock down myself anymore. Let me enjoy the power of freedom, let me speak up, let me do it myself." Aakash no more limits himself anywhere, be it at personal or professional places. He could unfold the secret of discovering himself.

We all have many personal goals. Many times, we don't prepare well to achieve them. And we find excuses to slip on. Aakash has seen many great teachers in his life. His father was the first one who showed him how impactful teachers could be for our society. Aakash always wanted to be a teacher. But, with an engineering degree and information technology industry experience, how would he meet that goal? In his profession, he tried finding out time and opportunities to impart trainings. As a trainer, he has been doing very well. Classroom is one such place, where you give your best and get back even more in return. There can't be a more fulfilling moment in your life than you as a faculty, interacting with many participants in a classroom.

Aakash wants to pursue teaching, post his retirement from information technology industry. Towards that goal, he spent two years completing his master's degree through a distance learning program. It requires strong will power to undergo a master's course while you are on a job, that demands most of your time and attention. Aakash worked hard to complete the course. When you are determined to succeed, your family's support is most important in your journey and Aakash considers himself very fortunate to be part of such a supportive family.

We all have an innate love towards music. Music is something that can cross all the barriers and touch our inner souls. Music can bring the best out of us, reminds us our past; and brings a fresh hope in our journey. Aakash and Camellia always wanted to learn a musical instrument. Why not start now? Both started attending guitar classes in the weekend. They went back to a new world of exploration, experimentation and engagement. Soon, they realized they have something else to get fun from. After six months, they started playing guitars together. Their son used to record them and upload them on social media. Encouragement and best wishes started flowing in. What makes Aakash even happier is the fact that Rayaan started playing guitar after seeing his parents' tireless efforts to make their dream a reality. Aakash is more convinced today that if you want something to happen, be at the front, do it yourself first!

We all need to have some attachment to something outside our primary work. That keeps us energetic and fresh in mind. That's where we get the needed mental support in difficult times. Rather than doing same old thing over and over, we need to find ways to keep ourselves charged.

Family First...

George Bernard Shaw said it long back, "A happy family is but an earlier heaven." Family is like a tree. However, we ignore it, it never stops helping us. Family is what keeps us moving in our lives. Family may not be just parents, siblings, spouses and children. Many times, our family is even further extended. Family is what keeps us bonded, always teaches us the first lesson, and defines purpose in our lives. We need to continuously nurture our family for us to have better fruits for our efforts. If our family is built on a solid foundation, we will always have the mental build to face any challenges. Together, we walk the journey, together we face it.

Aakash remembers his childhood when they had a larger undivided family. There were problems. When you have a small kitty and you need to share it with multiple people, you will have challenges. But even with all those odds, there was a sense of belongingness. There was someone to support you when you were broken. There was 'family' to encourage you to dream and achieve larger things in life. With time, our horizon keeps on changing. In a global world, people need to make a move to another place for earning. Personal touch starts reducing as we keep on trying to fit in a new environment. Communication gets lesser and lesser. We depend on social media to wish each other. More dynamic and busy we become; more distance comes in between. Meanwhile, many of our close ones leave us behind forever, with just memories.

In last 10-15 years, Aakash's family base has shrunk a lot. He no more has a choice to meet his grandmother, father and maternal uncle. He lost three of his closest ones already. His mother stays in his native place and Aakash lives in a different city, Hyderabad along with his wife and son. With Rayaan growing up, Aakash can hardly travel to his native place twice a year, just for a couple of days. His brother and sister got married and have settled in places around Kolkata. His uncle and aunty along with cousins have moved closer to uncle's office. Everyone has become too busy nowadays. The family is scattered and meet only on big occasions.

Aakash recently created a WhatsApp group for his family. Everyone got excited about the possibility with this app. They all came on a common platform where they could exchange information and updates with their happenings. People started posting pictures and wishing each other on birthdays, marriage anniversaries. Technology brought them together!

Aakash and his brother planned for a family trip to a beach town near Kolkata. After long time, they spent time together. There were many happy moments and they enjoyed a lot. They debated over very small things. When you spend time with your near ones, even a bit of fight brings a lot of love at times. Aakash and his family decided that all of them would meet at their native place during the upcoming *puja* vacation. His uncle showed a lot of energy even at this age for anything that brings them together. Aakash's mother and uncle directed the family as the senior-most members. Rest just went with the flow!

When it is all about near ones, the worth of gifts really don't matter. Aakash decided that he would gift all his near ones on their birthdays or marriage anniversaries. No price is enough to repay the debt, you have from your near ones. Still, every small gift conveys the message that we do care for each other, we wish the best for each other. Nowadays, we are so busy with our smallest family units, we forget many smaller things in life. A wish or a small gift reminds us that we are still together, however distant we might be. Gifts are our little gesture as a token of gratitude.

Human is becoming more complex as the civilization ages. In a competitive world, with struggling lives and materialistic aspirations, the human is facing tough challenges to nurture even the best gift in life, and that is relationships. We must do our part without any lapse in effort and contribution from our side. Life is too short, and nothing can be kept for future. We never know if we will get another opportunity again to see the smiles on the faces of our near ones. Does Aakash know what his brother loves to have? Does he still remember what makes her sister happy and excited? Does he remember what his uncle wanted him to achieve? Did he forget what his mother always used to advise him? Does he still remember why his sister made every effort to protect him in the society?

Whatever success we achieve in our life, nothing is of much value until we put every effort to keep our families happy. Nothing should take time away from our lives, such that we can't even meet each other couple of times in the year. Spending time with family is the best prize in our lives. We may not realize this during the peak time in our career. We all get into the race of success and that gradually becomes a race for survival. Meanwhile, we don't realize that couple of decades have already gone from our lives. We missed that caring touch that helped us to be here, we are today. Aakash took a resolution to take time from his busy schedule and stay in close touch with his family however distant they are now.

Back in Hyderabad, Aakash is living with his wife and son. Aakash understands that they are together in the same house but spending very less quality time with each other. When Aakash comes back home from office, usually Rayaan is all set to go to bed. When Aakash wakes up in the morning, Rayaan goes to school. They only get a chance to spend good time in the weekend. Aakash made some adjustments in his office schedule to ensure he spends quality time at home. We can't be productive without having a sustainable pace of work and balancing that with our personal lives. It is important to leverage the holidays to bring in fresh energy in our family. More importantly, we must contribute in activities at home, be it helping our spouse in household work, spending time with our children in the playground. I am sure, many of you would agree with me that at times, we should be fine to have a moderate performance rating at office, but we can't afford poor ratings from our family at home.

Aakash had planned few things with his family; they decided to do most of the things at home together when all of them are present. That could be cleaning home, cooking, having dinner, watching television, reading books, surfing internet, going for shopping and much more. When you start doing things together, you get the feeling of teamwork, rather than it being an individual effort. Even if you are going for an evening walk in the weekend, take your family with you. The most refreshing thing that we can do is walk together. We should look for opportunities to stay together and participate in everything, as we spend quality time at home.

We all are fascinated with some event or program. The Olympics is one such event, where athletes from many countries participate. More than winning medals; participation, the feeling of representing one's country is unparalleled. Watching people coming from across countries to support their nations is a lifetime experience. Did you ever imagine being in the Olympics village and hearing the national anthem? World Cup football is one of the greatest events on the planet. Our country may not participate, but all of us support some countries, or some footballers. These two events bring all the nations under one umbrella, igniting the inner sportsmanship spirits. Aakash and his family always wanted to see the World cup football and the Olympics once in their lifetime. Fortunately, the next Olympics and the world cup football tournament are happening in Japan and Qatar, which are not far from India. Aakash and his family are already making all the plans to make this dream a reality.

Another wish Aakash and family always wanted to experience but could not explore fully, was travelling. Every year, they usually go on a trip for one week. Aakash promised Rayaan that he, Camellia, Rayaan and Aakash's mother would go for two big trips in the next 3 years. The first would will be just after Rayaan's class tenth board examination. They would like to travel by car to some parts of Bengal in 2 weeks. The wish list had temple towns, dense forest, some old palaces, beaches on the Bay of Bengal and a portion of north Bengal with hills and tea gardens spread all over.

Bengal has all the gifts from God through plain land with green agriculture carpet, rivers across the state, rich heritage, beaches, forests, hill stations and whatnot. Aakash was excited about this trip to share moments with his mother, wife and son. The other trip that is always there in Aakash's mind is to travel across India, after Rayaan's class twelfth board examination. It would take minimum of a month and, Aakash was planning for money and time to see India from its beautiful pockets. The big-ticket places include the deserts and forts in Rajasthan, beaches of Goa, the beauty of Manali, green sugarcane farming in Punjab, The Taj Mahal, heavenly beauty in Kashmir, adventurous Leh and Ladakh and few more.

Rayaan was fond of physics and had a lot of curiosity for the universe and astrophysics. Aakash bought a physics lab kit to gift his son. Aakash was sure that his son got tones of pleasure to play with this lab kit at home. Aakash felt that it was not what he wanted to gift Rayaan, it was rather important to understand what Rayaan loved to receive. Few years back, Camellia took admission to a drawing class. Her teacher created lot of interest in her drawing aptitude. Aakash also motivated her to focus on drawing. She was deeply engaged in many creative activities at home.

Recently, Camellia started her classes for guitar as well. Aakash continued to motivate and support her in these areas. Everyone wants to achieve something in life. Peace of mind and a sense of happiness are keys to realize our aspiration. Let's support each other to grow and prosper. We can't walk long miles alone. We need partners and the first few ones are there at our homes only!

Bring Smile To Your Friends...

We all need friends, who will be there with us irrespective of our status, failure and accomplishment. While we need to keep us and our immediate family in good shape, we must pay attention to our friends who have been supporting and inspiring us since long when we were not what we are today. Aakash strongly believes that his childhood friends helped him dream BIG at a time, when the world was not that big to him. Lives in rural areas and that in urban cities are not the same. You don't get exposure to a bigger world in a small village. All you can get is a great family, supportive friends, guiding teachers and best of the friends. With time, as we get distant from each other, we must connect and know each other's state of mind, help them regain confidence in difficult times.

There is always a 'reality' factor that keeps on testing the foundation of any relationship. There is so much difference in family backgrounds, support, education, financial status and social identities. When Aakash looks back at the past, he can understand the gap. One of his friend's father used to do a daily labor job and his mother was more like a domestic help at his home. The problem was not with the kind of job they had. The amount of payment was not good enough for them to live a decent life. They did not have even money to have food twice a day. How would they have even thought of education, good clothes and a decent living?

It is not easy to grow up with a balanced mindset through such a difficult time. Naturally, they have not achieved a desired level of establishment in their professional and personal lives. The pain continues across generations until someone breaks the loop, stands up and establishes himself or herself. Unfortunately, many of Aakash's childhood friends could not. Even today, while Aakash and few friends are leading a decent life, some of their friends are still struggling with arranging food for their families.

Aakash keeps on wondering, when this would change. He could solve many problems in professional world but could never fix this one for near ones.

Aakash understood providing financial support once in a blue moon would not help his friends. In long run, this problem would only persist. Unless his friends stand up on a solid foundation, they would continue to face the challenges. It is great to see them having so much of respect towards life even when life is not that sweet to them. What can Aakash do about them? Does he have enough money to fund? He tried to understand what his friends could do with whatever skillset they had. Some of his friends were good at farming; some had got skills in painting furniture, while some were very good at cooking. It was just that they did not have enough opportunities. It was just that they were not properly paid for what they did every day. Aakash estimated how much funding they would need to establish businesses in their areas of expertise. He went to his village and called everyone for a meeting. He explained to them what kind of focus they needed to bring in for breaking all the barriers they had. For everyone, he made a realistic plan, showed them what they could start with and where they could reach with honest effort and hard work. Initially, his friends felt it was just another discussion. But this time Aakash was determined to make it happen. Behind the scene, he did a lot of groundwork to establish the base for each of the business units for his friends.

It was not big, rather small effort to have a foundation where someone could nurture further and make it bigger with time. Then a day came, Aakash invited all his friends.

They met together and Aakash handed over the small units to each of his friends along with a small letter.

My friends,

I *am sure all of you enjoyed a lot during our last trip to Darjeeling. It was truly going back to our childhood. I know time has taken away a lot from our lives. We have grown a bit older. We are not that fit and strong as we were 30 years back. We may not have that energy to go those extra miles to make each other smile. Trust me, it was still a great time to stay together again after a long gap. You know why; because you all were still same inside your hearts. We still had that naughty, childish minds. We still had fun pulling down each other. We still danced together on vengaboys music. We still were so competitive to steal that boiled egg when one was busy talking to another. We still had legs on each other in the bed while talking all through the night after that magical entertaining session.*

I can't believe we all were in the same coach in the sleeper class. We played cards together. Can you imagine the fun we had at night when one was sleeping deeply, and others were disturbing? I am sure our co-passengers did not like our naughty behavior at this age. The funny part was when we offered our apologies when the train stopped in Siliguri. Journey to Darjeeling was just amazing. Those few days seem to be like a dream. I can still see the scenes in the train compartment. In between breaks with tea and that white soft sweet sticks were so refreshing!

There was beauty was spread all over. But our minds had even more inside. The holiday home was as if made only for us. The lawn in front of the building was all green in the lap of Himalayas. It was breathtaking. We enjoyed every moment of it. I wish we could have more time. The goodbye moment instilled the appetite for our next meet. I know we became emotional that day for a while, but our tearful eyes whispered me we have not changed at all. We are still those old gold friends. Nothing could snatch away our friendships. I always believe we are human, if tears come in our eyes, when something touches our minds and hearts.

You remember, after those drinks that night, we were talking about our personal lives. Some of you hesitated to share the sad part of your life. Friends, how long will we only show our bright sides? I know we only want to offer smiles to each other. But at times, we feel relaxed to share our difficulties. I understood what you wanted to do and what was preventing you from achieving that. I could feel your pain of not accomplishing the goal that you have cherished all along. But I must tell you, no job is an inferior job. You all should be proud of what you are doing. You have got a great skillset in your respective areas. You are the experts! It is just that you are not paid that appropriately, as your skill deserves. The good thing is your families are supporting you a lot. They are always with you in your journey, a great blessing in life. You now must do something for your families.

Our friendship is based on a strong foundation. Our friendship came into our lives when we were nobody. There was no expectation, absolutely nothing. All we had was just a dream. I know you think I have become a considerably big guy. But I know I am not what you all wished me to be. Based on expertise you have built, and what you want to do, I planned for each one of you. I took time off from my office to focus on this project. After three months effort, they are now in much better shape, where you can start from and take it forward. I have confidence in you that you will be able to make it. So far, I was in pressure to live your dream. Now I give you something in return. Make it successful to make me happy. I know you all can!

I wish I could support much more. Forgive me as it took long time to extend this small help. You know nothing is that late, if we have that lifelong learner mind. You must be thinking where I got this money from? It's not my money, it's all yours. I will tell you later where I got this money from. For now, start your new life. Focus on your work. And never stop smiling.

Will not say Bye

Your friend, Aakash!

Aakash stayed back for a couple of more weeks with his friends. Aakash understands it may not be a big venture, but he realized that the small initiative has brought fresh air in their lives. The lost dream came back in their lives. So was the smile. This is what Aakash wanted to do since long. He wanted to give his best for his friends. He wanted to provide that initial support in their lives, which would work as a springboard for them to reach their goals. We usually believe we can help someone with just money. But trust me; more than money, time is precious. There is no better alternative than spending time together; because that's when you get to see the reality, the challenges and the opportunities to improve. Trying something on the ground is impactful. Life again started rolling on!

Past That Touched You Deep...

Have you ever come across a situation when you are travelling in a train or plane on a window seat and your mind leaves the seat, takes a tour through those distant trees or cloud and you reach your past in the memory lane? What do you see? As if, everything is happening again in front of you. Those moments and the characters touched us so deeply that even after decades you feel you still belong to those time slices. Why does this happen? Why does our mind turn back at times, though we are super busy with our present? The honest answer would be that people around us created a long-lasting impression in our minds. The impression was so deep that the toughest struggle or biggest accomplishment in our lives could not erase them from our mind-slates.

Aakash had the fortune to meet such people in his life. He always had the aspiration to meet them again. For some, he wanted to pass on his deep regards and respect. For some, he wanted to help them in however small endeavor it could be. Unfortunately, many of them are no more living on this planet. Two such personalities were his mathematics tutor and his chemistry teacher. Aakash was in class seven when he met his chemistry teacher for the first time. He was in his early fifties then. He had to use a hearing aid because of an ear problem. Every day, he used to come to school from a nearby village on a bicycle. During his ninth grade, Aakash used to attend his private tuitions. Outside Aakash's family, he was the first person who had injected the belief in Aakash's mind that he could do well if he worked hard. He had special attention towards Aakash in and outside the school. Outside studies, he used to spend a lot of time motivating him. In our lives, we are as successful as the scale is set before us. His chemistry teacher had set a very high target for Aakash during the childhood only. Through his eyes, Aakash could see the much wider world that was waiting for his arrival. In a remote village, it is not so easy to show a boy the path for future and help him connect to the road that takes him to the future of success.

Aakash had a wonderful well-wisher in the disguise of his mathematics tutor. He was a very strange personality. By profession, he was a businessman. Inside, he was a great mathematician. He was a socialist. Aakash heard that his mathematics teacher was very idealistic and a big fan of socialism during his college days. He was an active participant of the communism wave in Bengal during the eighties. When Aakash was in class ten, he had a lot of fear in mathematics. His father was worried about seeing his struggle in this subject. Aakash's father knew this mathematician and requested him to spend some time in the weekend to teach his son. This teacher was a very moody person. If he committed something, he would give his everything to make it happen. In the weekend, he used to spend almost four hours with Aakash. In the first one hour, he used to discuss a lot on society, economics, and international affairs. He used to share his thoughts with Aakash on the challenges in our country that were pulling us back from moving forward with all-round development for all people in the sphere. Aakash used to listen to him with much eagerness and respect. That one hour spent was like knowing the basics of life and having an appetite to do more for the society and people. Aakash's affinity towards social work was rooted long back in those days!

In three months, Aakash understood that mathematics is all about understanding the problem statement, identifying the available data points, and planning to use them in the right manner to reach the target outcome. His teacher made mathematics so easy for him that Aakash soon started playing with it like any other game. When you know something, even the difficult most actions look like the easiest one. Great teachers create interest in students' minds, show things in simplest way and encourage them to take on the challenges. Aakash could only get 3 to 4 months of time from his mathematics teacher. But that little time helped him in, not only solving mathematical problems, but also bring a wider perspective of life and meaning of true human impact in our society.

Aakash had tremendous respect for these two teachers. Unfortunately, none of them is alive today. Aakash even can't meet them. Aakash went to their homes, introduced himself to their families and paid regards and respect to his teachers. He took their blessings and came back home. After that, Aakash went to his own school and proposed to offer two awards for the highest scorer in mathematics and chemistry and dedicated those awards to his two great teachers. He also offered another two awards – one for the highest scorer in English and another for highest total marks and dedicated these two awards to the names of his father and grandmother. All four awards were for the students passing 10th grade board examinations. The awards were sponsored in the name of 'Yatra', the society that Aakash, his family and few of his friends had set up for overall development of education for the rural kids.

Aakash had a college batchmate named Aman. He never met him in the college campus. When Aakash went to his first job in mines, Aman also joined there. He was a very talented person and a true gentleman, an honest person. During those days in mines, they spent a lot of time together, be it inside the mine or in the officer's colony. He encouraged Aakash a lot during difficult times. Aakash still remembers it was Aman who first made him believe that he could also get into information technology job despite being a mining engineer. Aakash knows that it was god's blessings that he spent time with such a wonderful friend. He learnt many things from this friend, especially the patience, and keeping head cool in difficult times, respecting people even when you are challenged and more importantly, how to stay honest even during toughest times in life. He had a lot of influence on Aakash's life.

Aman is now a professor, teaching students in some college in northern India. Since long, Aakash had been thinking to meet him. Aakash and his family had planned for a family trip in north India and invited Aman and family to join as well. Together, they spent a fantastic time. They became very nostalgic, while discussing those mining days. Few days just passed by like lightning-fast moments. Aakash gifted him a manuscript and requested him to keep one day free in June when Aakash would come again to this city for his first book publication. There could not be a better moment than sharing the stage with such an inspiring friend.

If Aakash has learnt anything on people management and leadership skills, major credit goes to the DGM he worked with, in the mines. It was more than two decades; they had not met since Aakash left the job. Aakash could finally connect him through social networking site and he got to know that both live in the same city! In the Initial few weeks, they exchanged likes and comments on social media. Then Aakash planned to meet him in person at his residence. His DGM was now in the late seventies. With a lot of curiosity, he and his family went to his residence on one weekend. Aakash showed him his young-age picture and his DGM could recognize him. In minutes, they went back to those mining days. They cracked jokes, got to know each other's current situations. They discussed a lot on the current socio-economic situation and talked a little bit about the political state of the nation as well. Finally, Aakash tendered his regards and respect for him and family. He gifted a shawl, umbrella and manuscript of his first book. Aakash shared the summary of the story. His DGM's eyes glittered for a while. His professional hero was so happy to know that one of his juniors still follows his way of working together in a respectful manner. He could sense that his actions cultivated the picture of a 'true leader' in Aakash's mind and it is still there even after decades of wider professional experience across the globe. Aakash realized that his professional hero may have lost that brightness in those intelligent eyes, but the charming personality was still intact!

Another person Aakash still remembers is his old driver in Kolkata, Soham This person was from a very poor background but had a strong foundation of ethics that he inherited from his mother. Being a driver, he used to motivate Aakash a lot. He literally spent hours after hours to teach Aakash how to drive when he was so afraid to even hold the steering. He used to pay attention to Aakash's health and remind him to take medicines on time. In the idle time, he was the best friend for Rayaan when he was a kid. He brought in the aquarium that was very precious for Aakash during those days. Any place Aakash and family used to go, Soham always was there with them. In profession, he was a driver, but he was very close to Rayaan like his own uncle. Aakash helped him to buy a car that he could use in his profession. Unfortunately, he was cheated by the broker. Aakash understood that Soham was fighting against poverty for survival. Aakash went to his residence once, understood what they had and encouraged to give the land to a promoter. Soham got couple of flats and in some years' time, he became financially stable. Now, Soham has a bigger aquarium and a bigger space for the birds that he was always mad for.

Aakash did his part in a small way. He showed the path to Soham to move on. We need to ensure our surroundings also moves along as we move forward. We meet so many people in our lives. Many of them leave a permanent scratch in our minds. When we meet them, express our gratitude for all that they did for us, it brings lot of happiness and peace of mind. The love and affection that helped us grow; we must not leave them behind. Aakash could not meet all of them. But he is determined to try and do his best for these people, to whom he is largely indebted to and he knows he can't repay it in any form of sacrifice from his side.

Why do we limit ourselves to just a few people? Many times, we visit a place that stays in our minds forever. We see the strangers on the road or maybe, next door in the same hotel. Aakash wants to go to those places once more. He still wants to visit that village where he went for his first job. He wants to go to that small town in southern Indian state where he and his classmates went on vocational training during college days. He would love to ride a bicycle on that mud road, which took them to the movie theatre in the nearby town. He still wants to get the taste of those picnic days in their neighboring village, surrounded by canals and trees.

He still wants to walk that 8 kilometers to see the final match of his school. How about having those gatherings on the 100 feet road with his classmates? There are many such incidents that are still fresh in his mind. He knows time has passed by, in between. It won't be easy to get it back. Whatever form he can get them back, that is no less of satisfaction. Life is too short for us to wait for something. If your mind wants to touch something, go for it. Don't hold yourself back! Go and get it again!

Life is a journey across time slices. The same person behaves differently at different time slices and in different contexts. Controlling mind is important, as it takes control over us if we don't take care of it. Keeping cool and calm is key to success. If we want to achieve something in our lives, we first need to love ourselves, love our surroundings and people there. The happiness that it brings up paves the way for us to do even more.

Get, Set, Go....

How many times have you noticed that without doing anything, you have got drained out? How many times have you experienced that even after working the whole night, you still had loads of energy? That's the magical power of mind. Our mind sets the target before us. Many people across the globe even with disabilities have accomplished goals that sound impossible for them. They could do it because of their inner strength.

Different people have different sources of motivation. For some, the ability to gift the best to their nearest ones is the motivation. For few, arranging a meal a day for their families is the motivation. Everyone is driven by their respective source of motivation. That's what gets reflected in our work, lifestyle, behavior and outlook. Aakash has set very high expectations for himself; driven by the motivation to uphold the spread of humanity.

When one sets a benchmark for himself, it's hard to go off the track. Some unknown invisible force binds them to stay on track. Sometimes, it comes at a high price. No matter what happens in their lives, they must stand straight to nurture their own values. From the very beginning, Aakash hoped to try his best to bring back smiles on a few faces. In a larger world, that may be very small in scale; not really touching the lives of millions. But imagine the potential where we have thousands of 'Aakash' doing the same and those smaller efforts combined make this planet a much better place to live for millions! That's the motivation for Aakash. Nothing else attracts him more in life.

In the last few months, Aakash had paid attention to himself first. He gradually took out time to spend with his dear ones to see what make them smile. He did his best to help his friends move, one step forward in the journey of life. He connected people who guided him when he was just another 'nobody' with no individual identity. When you do something, you always have aspired for, it brings a lot of satisfaction in your mind and that sets you ready for chasing even larger goals in life.

Do we spend time to think what we really love to do? We all do a lot of stuff in our day to day lives. Most of the time, we do certain things as we need to do for our survival. We may not always realize that there are certain things we do very naturally, because we love them to do again and again. If we keep our eyes and ears open, we will be able to recognize them. All of us travel a lot these days. We notice some people are so eager to come forward, introduce themselves and start interacting with others. Why do they do so? Because they are very comfortable in connecting with others, that their views, understanding others' thought processes. They love it and that's why they do that so easily. If we are not comfortable, we won't open up, even if we strive from inside to speak up.

Our social behavior is very infectious. What we do, our nearest ones watch that, and it spreads beyond our knowledge. If we want our children to be social, first we need to be social enough. If we want our children to be fit, we need to set examples through us. If we do good things together and consistently, it brings a lot more enriching experience for all of us. This is more significant for common ordinary people. There are very few followers in their lives, unlike the celebrities. Common people have less opportunities to influence mass in doing positive things. The only way they can influence is by doing things together, leveraging combined effort.

Aakash aspired to bring changes in the way human thinks and acts. Being an ordinary person, he realizes that he, himself must set an example first and see all, he can attract to join him to do that consistently. If few people follow him and the effort gets multiplied over time, that's no way just an ordinary accomplishment! Aspiration is very strange in nature. They are situational as well. What we dreamt in our childhood may not push us forever to chase. At times, we may feel our box of achievement is full. But that is just a temporary feeling. Life moves on and we renew our goals as we continue to go through the steps of success and failure. There is no absolute conclusion, if we are what we wanted to be. Aspirations from past gets rebaselined as we continue with our journey. It is rather a better question to ask ourselves, if we are what we want to be.

Walk The Talk...

Some believe we chose to be who we are! Aakash wonders how many steps a human keeps on walking all through his lifespan! We all walk a lot. Every day, we keep on walking. Many people love to walk on the beach amid that soothing breeze. Some people walk that extra mile to meet their nearest ones. Few passionate people also walk to the peak of The Everest. Very few accomplished ones even walk in the space! Many people walk to keep themselves fit. And there are people who need to walk a lot, as they can't afford the transport cost. There are many other people who want to walk but can't anymore.

Aakash loves to walk. Not that he is very health concerned. He simply loves to walk when he feels so. Maybe that's when he talks to himself, that's what brings out the person inside in front of him. The great Indian Hindu monk, Swami Vivekananda advised us, "Talk to yourself once a day, otherwise, you may miss meeting an excellent person in this world".

Aakash still remembers that midnight twenty years back when he was coming from the mines in Orissa to his native place in Bengal. There was no bus or transport available that night. Only option was to walk 6 kilometers alone on the road to reach home. It was a completely isolated road with hardly any house or human around. Aakash walked that night alone, keeping the sky and moonlight as only witnesses. He could only see his shadow and hear his own footsteps breaking the silence.

Whenever Aakash feels a bit different, be it a happy or sad

moment, he has a habit of walking. He keeps on walking till his mind gets settled and wants to be back home. Five years back, he had decided to start the first day of the year with a walk. Many people have the belief that, what you want to do consistently, do it on the first day of the year! You welcome the year with lot of energy and strong determination. Aakash was wondering how many kilometers to start with. To his surprise, he decided to walk one kilometer extra than the last two digits of the year. It was 2015 and on the first day of the year, he walked 16 kilometers. The experience was so refreshing! His mind turned to be magically clear and balanced. As if someone has cleaned his mind and there was no doubt left there. He shared the accomplishment with some of his friends and they encouraged him a lot. It was no less than an achievement in his life! That's how Aakash started something new. On the first day of the year for the next few years, some unknown force inspired him to do this again and again. Every time he was walking one kilometer extra. That one kilometer was telling him, "Yes Aakash, you can still walk to the next year!"

This is year 2020. This time Aakash started for 21 kilometers in the morning of 1st January. Aakash decided to come live on social media while he was walking. He shared the story behind his 'walk' and wished everyone a very happy new year. Within minutes, he received many likes and comments with loads of encouragement. Within hours, he started receiving calls from many known people whom he had not been in direct touch, for almost a decade. Many shared their wishes to start walking from next year. It was so accomplishing! There was no medal for this achievement. But the glow on his son, Rayaan's face said it all! He was walking for last 5 years all alone. This year also he did it alone. But when it did spread, Aakash realized next year on the first day, he won't be alone anymore!

Aakash started planning for the next year. He named

the event as 'Walk YY+'. Many of his colleagues and friends in the city volunteered to walk 22 kilometers the next year. They planned to take donations, print t-shirts with caption "Walk YY+ in 2021". They decided to provide wheelchairs to few who couldn't walk. Aakash understood the significance of setting examples and doing things together. Next year, hundred people would walk together, and few persons would get on the wheelchair! A time would come when Aakash won't be able to walk anymore, but he is sure on 1st January every year, many people would come on the street to reach 'Walk YY+' target. Aakash is hopeful there will be people around the world who would walk 100 kilometers on 1st January 2099! And it would be great when those few people on wheelchairs would also participate!

Back 2 Pathshala...

It was just another day in office for Aakash. He was seriously looking into a deliverable. It was a last-minute final review before the submission. In the middle of a serious review, his cell phone rang. Aakash reluctantly received the call. There was an unknown voice on the other side. He addressed Aakash with his nick name. Aakash understood the person must be someone from his school or college days. The other person kept on saying, "I called you to share my little accomplishment today. I got a job as a teacher in a nearby school. I know my sir is no more there. He was the person who motivated us a lot during our school days. I thought even if I can't tell my sir, at least let me share the good news with his son. I am sorry to disturb you. But I could not resist myself. Please take my regards. I am sure I have the blessings from my sir."

For a while Aakash was spellbound! He knows his father did a lot in that school and village. But his father had left forever, twelve years back. And this student still remembers him! Who says people easily forget everything? Aakash's mind went back to his father's school. He could see his father talking to the students in the teachers' room. He could hear his father's words, "I know this is a small village. You all may not be that privileged in terms of richness, status and support system. I urge you all to dream for future. Work hard, pay attention to real education. One day you all will be reaching your destination". Aakash was a little boy to understand his father that time. Today, he realized that some of those students understood that day and followed what his father said!

In our lives, there is a lot of difference amongst people, their backgrounds and support systems. Everyone may not be coming from well off established background as few others. There may be barriers to flourish. We all can overcome them, if we have a dream and we are motivated to achieve them whatever may come on our ways. We all need someone to encourage us, some examples before us to follow. Couple of years back, Aakash started 'Yatra' mission in rural areas of Bengal. He used to go to those villages' education centers. He used to spend time with the kids there. Those kids were from very ordinary background. Aakash used to share stories with them. He still remembers those faces. They started believing in themselves, dreaming and getting ready for their futures. A little bit of motivation could bring in so much of positive vibe in our minds!

Aakash usually finds time to take sessions in his corporate life. Teaching is something he always wanted to pursue. He takes up these sessions very seriously and leaves no opportunity for making meaningful connects in the classroom. But that's all about our professional world. There are many people in this world outside this corporate fence. There are many students who have merit and skills, but badly need someone to ignite their motivation lamp. It is not just the syllabus or formal education that helps our students to contribute in the society. Our moral characters are built during those school days. Students need to be shown the right path and direction. Once they are motivated, they will automatically excel. Parents don't need to run behind them for studies, and more studies.

Can't Aakash start again reaching out to those students? Even if a handful students are encouraged, that's a great accomplishment. Aakash made a list of schools. Of course, his own school was at top of the list. He made a few slides' presentation with visuals and examples. His intent was to show the real value in life and how that motivates us to move in the right direction in our journey. He took some living examples, who bring in so much positive changes in our lives. He wanted to help the students visualize a much bigger world, motivate them dream and achieve their aspirations. The platform was all set for a new journey with next generation!

Then one day, he went to his Alma Mater and spent the whole day with the students showing the possible future in front of them. The students initially reacted a bit different when they saw something outside the syllabus. Gradually the day brought in a lot of fun in the class. It was truly a different day for Aakash and gave his best in the session. He cared to answer each curious question. He encouraged everyone to come out of the shell and try honestly to reach their goals. It was a very nostalgic moment for Aakash. It was the same school and same classroom, where he also had started his journey like the many current students.

Aakash got to understand the difference between corporate minds and the youth in a school. He prepared well to create interest in the young minds. His determination to do more got wings. He planned to conduct similar sessions in his known schools, especially in his father's school and the school, his father served as secretary for some time. With every session, he was enhancing the experiential quality. He started applying his learning from each session. In the first six months, he took similar sessions in ten schools. He could touch the lives of a thousand students!

But in a big country how many schools could Aakash cover? How many students would he get opportunity to interact with? There must be similar minded people who would be eager to come forward and contribute. Aakash created an online club called 'Back 2 PathShala'. There he started sharing his initiative, pictures and videos of the sessions. Aakash came in touch with many people, shared his experiences with the students. Many of them soon started taking similar sessions in their known schools. When good stories are shared, the spread of positive vibes multiples soon. Aakash was again convinced, “There are many ‘Aakash’ on this planet who are ready to walk that extra mile to help each other. We only can multiply that number through our active involvement, contribution and sharing”.

Care For Equality And Inclusion...

We all care for our child. Every day, we pray for their wellbeing. We work hard to support their present and secure the future. We feel happy or sad on their success or struggles. Every parent tries their best to support their child. Everyone is not born with same fortune though. While some children get the needed support, many are deprived of basic needs in their early lives. While it is great to think of it, solving the issue is not an easy task. We all belong to different social and economic cluster depending on many factors, such as background, support and readiness, opportunity, timing, hard work and many more. Even though we try to be a bit of socialist, the difference would always remain. Maybe, the disparity ignites the fire inside us to do more, to do better.

There was an aunty who used to work as domestic support when Aakash was a teen. She used to take care of many things in their family. In hot summer day or shivering winter night, she was always there to help. She used to do it for a minimal wage. She had four children and was finding it very difficult to even arrange for their meal twice. Aakash noticed many times, she used to take the food back home so that her children could have it. Aakash's parents sometimes used to give her the clothes and books, when they were no longer needed for their children. It was nothing compared to what the aunty needed. But this small gesture also used to help her to some extent. No help is small as such!

Even today, the picture has not changed much. Of

course, the world has advanced a lot. Human civilization has witnessed considerable evolution and development in day to day life. Many great people have come on this planet and they brought in tremendous change in the way humans think and act. Many organizations are working towards overall development of our societies. There is still a lot to do to bring the balance in our socio-economic circle. In countries like ours, there is a need to support people working in unorganized sectors, like our domestic helps. While we encourage people to do their own work, a considerable percentage of people manage their livings through jobs like domestic help with very minimum wages. These people even cannot ask for vacation. There is no labor law for this population, at least not known to many common people.

Many domestic helps bring their kids along with them, just because there is none to take care of them at home in their absence. We take care of our kids and we are fortunate enough to be able to do this. We buy books and clothes for our children. What do we do with those clothes and books when they are no longer needed or useful after few years? We can give those to our domestic helps for their children. Camellia has been doing this since some time. Whenever something is a bit old and not that needed for Rayaan, she usually gives those to our domestic help. Camellia thought of doing this even at a bigger scale. There are around 1000 families in their community. She connected some of her neighbors and explained the benefits of collecting the used books and clothes and hand them over to hundreds of domestic helps who come to their community every day. If their children get some support, they can also live a decent life. Can't we extend our helping hands a little bit more?

To her joy, Camellia observed that many of her friends in the community came forward to contribute. They brought the old books, clothes and handed over to the children of many domestic helps. What was getting wasted in their lofts for several years, was now set to bring smiles to many young faces. Then came the mobile app to drive this initiative digitally. Residents could register in the app and opt to donate the used clothes and old books for the domestic helps in their own communities. Camellia was so happy to see that her little effort had spread, and many communities came forward to help the children of their domestic helps.

We don't always realize that there are a lot of things, wasted after some years of use. If we treat every child as ours, we must be acting not to let those waste anymore. We could be a bit more organized to help those who are not as privileged as our children are. A little bit of care and support could bring in many changes in our surroundings.

Human Touch To Resolve Conflicts...

We have seen conflicts since the pre-historic ages. This is not something we can eradicate completely. Even the best of the friends gets into conflict for reasons unknown, at times. We see conflicts amongst the brothers, colleagues. Conflicts in interest may be there in office, society, family gathering, political party, government and beyond. Conflicts may cross the border of the nations as well. Conflicts usually arise because of difference in opinion, difference in interest, distraction due to ego, fear of losing benefits and many others. History witnessed conflicts across geographies, amongst people with varied social status, financial strength. Conflicts may come between people with different races, languages, political beliefs, religions and castes across geographical regions.

If we further zoom in to any conflict, it happens mostly due to the loss of trust. Even at home, small things, if not handled with care, lead us to a long running misunderstanding and conflict. The dearest one becomes distant suddenly. Friend becomes an enemy. The known one starts behaving like an unknown. Day by day, people are getting restless. Often, we are so much frustrated, we forget that we are in a public place and don't exhibit true human behavior. Even the most gentleman loses patience due to tremendous pressure in our day to day lives.

Aakash knows one family that spent four decades in property related conflicts with their neighbors. They kept on fighting with their neighbors to forcefully occupy a small piece of land. Aakash really wonders what they actually got in the process! Because of their behavior, their next generation hardly got any opportunity to mingle with the fellow people. Now with the passage of time, those family members have started to fight between themselves to capture the property. It just turns out to be a habit of getting into conflicts. They just need something to stay busy with.

In childhood, Aakash witnessed many terrific conflicts between political parties, and believers of different religions. Be it politics or religion, some people play the spoilsports. For their individual gains and selfish nature, they spread hatred and common people get carried away very easily. Of course, with the advent of education, economic growth and thanks to media, these kinds of conflicts are gradually decreasing. Percentage of people with sensible minds has increased. In such a populous and diversified world, there are still many people, groups who find opportunities to create differences and spread rumors to ignite devastating conflicts.

As a human, we must be sensitive to each other's emotions. We must leave behind all ego and negative feelings to resolve conflicts in a peaceful way. We are here just for a few years. Nothing is permanent in our lives, nor would we stay on this planet forever! Why don't we just focus on well-being of common people? No religion or political party wins unless humanity wins. South African anti-apartheid revolutionary, Nelson Mandela taught us long back, "No one is born hating another person because of the color of his skin, or his background, or his religion. People must learn to hate, and if they can learn to hate, they can be taught to love, for love comes more naturally to the human heart than its opposite."

The bigger issue is that people who directly get involved in the conflict do never really get anything out of it. In pockets of this world, people don't have the freedom of speech and vote. Some handful people try to control societies with muscle power. Their bread and butter come through their blind support to the political leaders. When will that change? Can education or jobs change these people? When can we throw out these political leaders who divide people in the name of religion, caste? When will we get those leaders who would take us to the right path and work selflessly for the people, society or the nation?

We are such a big nation. We had so many great people who have made our country proud. We still have plenty of wise people who are trying their best to make this country even greater. Still, why do we have so many conflicts? Is it because of our education system that is not teaching us the basic values in life? Is it poverty taking a stab in our moral values?

Is it the evil forces taking super shading over the good people? Or is it just that we don't have self-respect and feeling for a united civilized nation?

Time has come for our education system to be re-designed to teach us basics of humanity. We need to focus on true education, rather than just certification and cracking entrance tests. Good citizens need to stand up and be vocal to safeguard our nation. We must create an environment where we can continue to stay together in harmony. We don't need to focus too much on which religion we belong to, or which political ideology we believe in. We have many great virtues, despite challenges and differences. Our outlook could be better through our consistent efforts.

Why do we need to apply force to control various movements in the world? Why are some people picking up arms to go against the administration? It is not matching with the ideology that Mahatma Gandhi had shared with us long back. Our societies need to be more inclusive. Whatever differences there are, we must thrive to resolve the conflicts. If any government or society accepts every span of its citizens, treat them equally, we hope not to apply force to retain the unity in our oneness.

Aakash personally wanted to visit those forests and hilly areas where tribal people were struggling with their livings. He wanted to stay with them and facilitate social upliftment programs and government funds in those remote places. He visited many such places, identified many similar minded people. He explained to common people that there was no way to peace, peace was the way. We have many NGOs spread over the country. We must create an environment where government and NGOs could start initiating the development programs. Leaders must come forward to engage with these organizations for betterment of the people.

Aakash always wanted to visit Kashmir, the heaven of India. The government, NGOs and private companies were working together to make people's lives better. If people have education, infrastructure, jobs, why would they not be part of the mainstream? Love and affection increase the national feeling and brotherhood. Recently, prime minister of our neighboring country said, they had defeated us multiple times in cricket during his time. Aakash was a big fan of this legendary cricketer turned politician. His skills and leadership on the ground were exceptional. Even if they had defeated us, we had respect for him as a cricketer. He should mark similar achievement as a political leader first to get respect from India. We are working in India to uplift the society for people's welfare. Rather than thinking of wars, he would do better to make his countrymen truly humane and prosperous. If that happens, he does not need to call out for fights with us anymore. We are happy to compete in nation-building, development and people welfare, not the hatred.

Be Part Of Solution, Not Pollution...

Few days back, we got to know that Bengaluru was the most traffic congested city in the world according to a report released by a location technology company. There were three other cities in India featuring amongst the top ten most traffic congested cities globally. Anything wrong with these cities? There could be multiple reasons. In India, middle class segment expanded exponentially in last one or two decades and many families have multiple cars. Insufficient roads and their bad condition could be another factor as well. It could be due to insufficient traffic management logistics. Even the reason could be improper planning of the city. It could be because of many other surrounding towns and villages, being more and more dependent on these cities. Whatever be the reason, ultimately people are spending more time on roads instead of real work. It is leading to more fuel consumption, more pollution. It is limiting people's abilities to reach their destinations on time. Sometimes, we see people being restless on the road, end up having accidents. They are getting exhausted even before taking up the actual work assignments.

These are good topics to be discussed over a cup of tea during the break hours in offices. Aakash and his friends were as usual, debating on this. Most of them have got cars. One of their colleagues usually come to office by public transport. He has yet not bought a car, though he could afford it well. Aakash asked him about the problem and his point of view. He said, "I know we all are busy, and we need to have flexibility in coming and leaving office based on our schedule. Owning a car is helpful as it provides us a lot of flexibility. However, I never felt that not having a car limits one's ability to work. I still come to office at the right time, do my work and leave the office at decent time. It not only helps me save money, more than that, I have less headache of driving in such a traffic congested road. I am satisfied that I am not contributing much in fuel consumption or pollution. The way my family travels for day to day work, I do the same way. There is an equal living standard for all in my family".

Aakash and his friends initially were joking with this colleague. Some even said, "How much more money would you want to save?" Very soon, they realized he was doing the right thing. But how would they handle their day to day unpredictable schedules without having a personal car? One of their colleagues was physically challenged and she could not drive a car. But she was one of the best performers in the team. That revealed the fact that to perform your duty and job, you don't need to necessarily drive your personal car to be super flexible.

One of Aakash's colleagues suggested that they could give it a try. They all looked at their office calendar and understood that on two days in the week, they had fewer meetings in the morning and evening hours. They decided that these two days in the week, only two persons would bring the car and other 6 persons could avail a pickup and drop facility. Rest of the days in week, they would avail the office buses. With this option, they started enjoying connecting with each other in the car and even in bus. The boredom during the journey while in traffic was gone like a magic. They didn't get exhausted so easily anymore. Additionally, together they saved three thousand rupees in a week. They started contributing this money to CSR activities in office.

Aakash and his colleagues together, were almost a 300 members team. At least 10 percent of this population were coming to office by their own cars. They tried to spread this small initiative to the wider team. When all of them joined hands, together they saved fifty thousand rupees a month. They started utilizing a portion of this money to drive cleanliness in their localities. Limiting one problem helps us focusing on other problems. Did Aakash and his colleagues ever imagine the potential of such an impactful initiative? We all can do small things with great passion, and when that multiplies, that leads to even larger impact to our society. Common men can bring in many changes in the way we live our lives. There are lot of opportunities to improve. The choice is ours!

Save Our Souls...

If I may ask you, what do you consider as the best gift in your life? I am sure we will have thousands of different answers. Situations, personal tastes and even necessities make gifts so dear to all of us. Even if we put a disclaimer, "Gifts are not encouraged at all...", we all feel special with that nice gift. Some parents feel that their child is the best gift, GOD has given to them. Many even feels, this planet itself is the most precious gift.

Long back when Aakash was probably in primary or junior secondary school, there was a teacher in his school. He was a teacher of Physics. Aakash never had an opportunity to attend his classes. This teacher was most probably one of the very few persons, who was trying to bring in lot of positive changes in that village. He used to stay in the teachers' hostel and in the weekend, he made it a point to spend quality time with the local children. He taught the children to be disciplined, to stay fit. He prepared them for cultural programs. More than three decades back, he showed those children in the village, how they could improve and do better in our extra-curricular activities through focused learning. Soon, he became very popular and started facing challenges from the conservatives in the village. Before he left the village, he encouraged all the students to go for plantation around the school premises.

Aakash is no more in touch with this teacher. Few months back, when Aakash had gone to his school's centenary year celebration, to his pleasure, he saw those small trees had grown big now. They were still standing high with their heads upright and branches spread wider. Aakash smiled realizing that his physics teacher had given the best gift to the villagers and left a long-lasting impression. We all know the climate change and its possible impact on this planet, to its living beings. Urbanization is expanding much faster than what could be imagined. In the backdrop of this real threat, there could not be a better gift than planting a tree. Long back our ancestors used to worship trees as GOD. That brought in lot of regards, respect and care for trees. In the last few decades, country like India has seen much of a mindful drive through plantation and 'save water' initiatives. Huge population in a country like ours can bring changes in both positive and negative ways. Choice is ours. It is good that our countrymen decided to go for plantation, and we can see the fruits today.

What difference can we, the so-called common people, bring in? Can't we plant at least one tree in our lifetime? Few days back there was a pleasant news in some of the leading dailies in India. One common person started planting in a desert like place. Over the years he continued to do so and ended up planting thousands of trees in that locality. He is a real-life hero! We must salute him for his tireless. Many times, the experts comment that population is a big barrier in true development of our country. But it could be our strength as well, if wisely utilized. We all can plant at least one tree in our lifetime. If we all do that, we can easily add 100 crores of trees in our country itself.

What's the point in just 'sitting and waiting' for others to act? There are many things we can contribute as individuals and when they are summed up together, that leads to a great revolution. We all can start saving water at home, in office, schools as much as possible. Aakash started gifting a tree on birthday or anniversary celebration in his known circle. Initially, it looked bit strange but once the tree grew up with a bit of care, the recipient of the gift felt very proud and satisfied. After a decade, when we would grow up further and observe that tree has grown up as well, that's the best gift we can have in our lives!

Greta Thunberg is a living example and inspiration to many of us in current generation. She has shown us that nothing can stop us in making impactful contribution. Being a teenager, she is leading campaigns for environment and urging immediate action to address the climate crisis. She does not want to wait for tomorrow for great things to happen. Aakash thinks many young minds are following her across the globe and the good things can only multiply over the time. There could be many more Greta around the world. Not that everyone would be able to impact at that scale. However, every individual effort will multiply and lead to a mass change on this planet. Many people on this planet still remember that Argentina won the 1986 soccer world cup. After decades, many of us might have forgotten who had scored the winning goal. What matters today is that Argentina won that world cup. That world cup became famous for legends like Maradona, Platini and few other greats. But at the end of the day, it was soccer that won people's hearts.

Aakash strongly believes, personalities like Greta are those individual heroes, who inspire the teams, the whole generation to do more and help others to be part of the winning team. Let us put all our efforts to make our generation a winning team in managing climate crisis. And the best gift for current and future generations could be saving water and more plantations. Let us start doing it today, as an individual, as a group in our family, in our society, schools, office, almost everywhere, where we can reach. We all can follow Mother Teresa's footsteps – "I alone cannot change the world, but I can cast a stone across the waters to create many ripples". We all can contribute to protecting the environment and help our current and future generations to live in a better planet.

It Is Our Society, We Need To Build It...

The current generation is heavily influenced by data or information. Thanks to social media, press, internet and mobile, we have access to all possible information. When we switch on the television or glance through the newspaper, we understand that some or another unpleasant incident are happening every day across the globe. It pains us all when we see issues with women's safety; we feel helpless but can't do much about it. Every day across the globe, some child is forced to embrace labor work, sacrificing his or her childhood. Many families are burning inside with the burden of dowry. We see a lot of inequality cornering us every day and gender inequality always appears at the top of this list. And how many years will we continue to surrender to extremists? On top of that, our society treats people based on the kind of jobs they are doing. Established professionals are given due respect and wages. People, who are doing skilled labor jobs, are not treated well at all. And we continue to claim (not believe), "All jobs are equal; people must not be differentiated based on the gender or jobs they are into!"

This does not mean there is nothing good in our society. Rather, only a few pockets of people are engaged in wrongdoings. Those incidents drag our society down in the eyes of the wider world. Anytime some mishap happens, question marks come on administration quite obviously. Unfortunately, behind all these bad incidents, there is a hidden human being only! Who are to be blamed for this? Is it because of a lack of proper education? Is lack of acceptance from the society and imbalance in social status making these humans so inhumane? Or is degraded morale value causing these nuisances?

If there are wrongdoings, there are always people to stand up and do human justice. We are living at a time, where there is no dearth of talented human beings. Their cumulative power is extremely strong. We just need to encourage people to do more and be examples for others. Aakash still has few childhood friends in his village. Some of them are working, some are doing businesses. Some of them are in fact leading various social initiatives. Good news is that some of his friends are established there as political leaders. Aakash wanted to connect similar minded people to join hands with him to drive some of the initiatives.

With lots of hope, Aakash went to his village. He met a few friends and spoke about his initiative. Some of them were very excited and showed interest to contribute actively. Then he called for a meeting with his known people and friends. He shared the blueprint. He explained, "We have many challenges in our society. Women need to feel secure and need to be respected. No child should be left behind, and we must stop child labor. We need to campaign against the curse of dowry. No father or brother should feel helpless with the burden of dowry. All families need to treat their children equally. A girl must not be treated amongst 'secondary priorities'. We must create awareness to let people know the serious consequences of extremism." He paused for a minute. Everyone was looking at his face. Aakash said, "Do you think these are issues that our village is still living with? Do you think we can do our part to stop or at least reduce it?" His friends agreed and asked, "How do we do it?"

Aakash smiled and replied, "I left the village more than 2 decades back. You all still came forward today when I invited you. You are the faces of this village. I am sure many of our fellow people will follow you and join us when they see you on the front. Let's be confident that we will do it." He continued, "I have a plan to go to our schools and conduct awareness sessions on social problems. We will hand-pick students who will be part of our initiative." One friend said, "We can invite few more men and women from the society, who want to contribute for the society. We can involve some of the senior citizens, who can guide us. Together, we can form a great team to start this initiative."

As they discussed, they immediately acted. Aakash personally went to couple of schools and identified few bright students who had an appetite to do for the social causes, very similar to what Aakash had during his childhood. They got some good citizens to join them. They divided almost 100 members into 5 different committees to handle five problems that Aakash had shared with this group. Each committee had the right blend of men and women, young and seniors, educated and uneducated, servicemen and businessmen. In the initial few days, Aakash shared his thoughts and explained what is expected from each of the committees. He said, "The minimum expectation is that you as individual must be setting example yourself to proudly say you are a member of this committee."

Very soon, these committees started raising funds from the well-wishers. They arranged for multiple awareness sessions in the village. Girls were taught to be confident and self-sufficient. Parents were invited to workshops to share that girls and boys are equal, and we must not differentiate them in aspect. Boys and men were invited in the workshops to remind them that the way they respect women at home, they need to behave the same way even outside. Every woman is someone's daughter or sister or spouse or mother. If we respect them, we are ensuring respect for our own family's women as well. The committee members arranged for campaigns against child labor. They explained to common men that religion itself is not damaging us. It is few extremists who are dividing our society in the name of GOD. Each family was given a leaflet to campaign against the curse of dowry system. What is the point of marriage, where dowry determines the course of the post-marriage life?

In six months, Aakash realized few people left the group. But to his surprise, many new faces had joined them. The good news was that many young men and women actively participated. Many senior people gave their blessings and guidance. Many well-wishers came forward with financial support. The whole village underwent a wave of change. This does not mean the whole society was purified suddenly. There were still some people who were finding opportunities to bring down this initiative. There was still insecurity in women's minds in pockets. Maybe, in some families, people were still taking dowry. But there were many people who stood up against these curses in society. Aakash noted down the achievements of these heroes and published their stories on the 'Yatra' website.

Aakash's friends could bring in lot of changes in the way the villagers were living their lives so far. When ten motivated sincere people join hands, they could defeat the bad intent of hundreds of people. When ten people stand up for the right cause, thousands others follow them. Aakash is hopeful that many other villages, societies can learn from what his own village is doing. Many inspiring social initiatives can even start from the remotest village. We, the common people can make a lot of difference on this planet. It is just a matter of someone taking the initiative!

Let Children Live Their Childhood...

Nothing is perfect in this world. We all go through different situations and create our own perspectives of various elements in our life.

Aakash's childhood was in no way, different. Most of his friends were from struggling families. Many of his friends had to sacrifice education in their early childhood and jump into work for the earning and welfare of their families. We all want children to be able to focus on studies or any other fields that they love to do. Forcing a child to do anything against their will and taking their childhood away from them is a crime. There is a fine line of difference in our perspectives as well. Parents can tell the children what is right and wrong, even if the children don't like it. In a family, it's okay if the children help their family in whatever way without impacting their childhood experience.

Aakash had a friend who was never that interested in studies during his early days. He was from a family where the seniors used to earn through agriculture and masonry work. He dropped out of school and started working in a bicycle repair and services shop. He worked there for one year without any wages or stipend. While Aakash and other friends were busy with studies, sports, swimming and lots of other fun, he used to work hard to learn how to repair or assemble parts of a bicycle. He did not even have time to come to the playground. Naturally, he could not make that bonded friendship with other children.

After a decade, that friend became a businessman and

one of the influential people in their society. After Aakash and many of his friends left the village for work or higher education, he took the lead and continued with the social events and programs in the locality. Today when Aakash or his friends come to the village, his bicycle shop is the place where they meet. He is married now, financially well placed and his daughter goes to an English medium school. After decades, Aakash realizes, this friend has been the most sincere and genuine human being despite that he missed his childhood education. Aakash had another junior friend who also worked hard in the childhood and established himself later in the business. Interestingly, these two friends always showed lot of interest to know the larger world through Aakash's experience. Their willingness to learn has been unparalleled.

Today, every parent is trying to offer their kids all that they possess. That's why we see so many successful young folks coming up in different fields from various segments of our society. It is no more a surprise when we see someone cracking an IIT entrance or civil services examination, even if none from his or her family had gone to college or university before. Many young people from very poor background are representing our country in the field of sports. That's the new generation! They are here to overcome all the odds and move forward.

We continue to wish that every child must be getting food, clothes, a home, healthcare and basic education. There are many governmental and non-governmental organization initiatives aimed at providing better quality and experience to the lives of millions of underprivileged children. Many times, common people even are not aware of these social benefits. We all can help these families and children by spreading awareness and helping them to avail these benefits.

While there are initiatives to provide the much-needed

support to the children, there are many other problems that today's children are facing. With the globalization spreading its arms, people are moving to urban areas. Families are becoming more nuclear. Parents are busy with their jobs and professional world. On one side, we see children are not getting space in slums. They cannot afford to have a decent living. On the other side, some children in a luxurious apartment even have none at home to talk to them.

With none around, children are spending more time on television, internet, mobile apps and games. There is lot of pressure and expectations to meet. Every day, every moment, kids are being compared. There is an emotional breakdown for these children. Children are being bullied everywhere. There is always uncertainty and fear of losing. They can still sustain with less food and luxury. But they can't withstand the pain of domestic violence. Children need to be provided peace of mind. These are much bigger problems than lack of food, clothes or basic education.

Whatever problems a child goes through, and however difficult life is, children need support, encouragement and more importantly, someone to spend time with. Aakash and his family introduced a section in their society 'Yatra' homepage. This is where any child could ask questions for help and guidance. Rayaan created a youtube channel for spreading awareness on childcare and various social benefits schemes. Aakash and a few of his friends went to remote places and started taking workshops on good parenting. There was lot of participation; many women came forward to know and share more. Children also learnt many new things.

If we all pay attention to our own circles and take some time to contribute, today's children would have a much more fun-filled childhood. Even our own children would come forward to help other fellow children. They are the future of any nation, and it is very critical for all responsible citizens to create a better environment for our children. Today's children, when they grow up, will take the society to the right path. Together, we can make this planet a better place to live for every child!

Terrorism: Let's Join Hands To Uproot The Menace...

Our country and neighborhoods are some of the biggest victims of acts of terrorism. Twenty-first century woke up with the deadliest terror attack in the USA. The whole world witnessed how organized these terrorist organizations had become over time. India has been suffering from this menace for long and had been voicing about this on international forums. Very few developed countries understood the widespread impact on humanity due to terrorism. It is now evident that terrorism does not have any boundaries. Over the past decade, an average of 20,000 people has been victims of terrorism worldwide each year. Terrorism is often focused in certain regions. Within these regions, concentration varies across specific countries. The middle east and northern Africa have experienced most deaths due to terrorism in 2017. South Asia and Sub-Saharan Africa also had high death tolls in the same year. In South Asia, most deaths occurred in Afghanistan, with high numbers in India and Pakistan as well. Analysts say acts of terrorism are usually aimed at attaining a religious, social, political, and economic goal.

People across the globe are very concerned about terrorism. Some of the developed countries are in a "global war on terror" post the September 11 tragedy. This war is not limited to any one specific country or region. There is no data-supported evidence on the number of casualties. But some global bodies estimate the number is approximately 3 million through direct and indirect deaths. Do you remember how big of an economy India is? Currently, it is at 2.8 trillion US dollars. China is with 14 trillion and USA is with 21 trillion US dollars economy. You all know that Apple recently became the world's first trillion-dollar company. And to run such long-running 'war on terror', it costs around 5 to 7 trillion US dollars!

What is the big accomplishment of terrorists in killing innocent people? What are those few nations even gaining in the war against terrorism? At the end of the day, these wars are also killing millions of people at the expense of trillion dollars. If you see the world map, there are numerous pockets where separatists are running a proxy war against the state and its people. At the same time, some states are supporting and sponsoring these separatist movements in the name of support for "freedom fight" and support for "human rights". Most of the developed and developing countries are spending 2-4% of their GDP on military expenditure. Do common people support this? Who is gaining in the process?

Most of the people across the globe believe that terrorism must be rooted out to its entirety. No civilized society supports this menace. There is no bravery award for these cowardly acts of terrorism. It is a shame that some people are carrying out these acts of hatred against the very own humans. Will they ever realize that their act is killing some brothers, sisters in this world? Do they understand even their nearest and dearest ones will hate them when they see such cruel, shameful acts?

Forget these terrorists. They are just humans in blood and flesh. They may not have true human genes in their hearts and brains. The question remains, how do we stop this? Can 'war on terror' really uproot this and throw it out of this planet? Aakash recently started a blog on this topic. His blog reached out to thousands of people across countries. He received many suggestions and ideas from different generations of people. While some people still believe that such a dark episode should be finished through a tough stance by the superpowers, many think there are better ways to handle it. Aakash is optimistic that the global powers and their leaders may get a lot of inspiration and motivation from these common people across the globe. Aakash wanted to share their thoughts. Who knows? Someday some leader may hear out these global citizens and act as true global leader in resolving the menace.

Let us hear the first voice of a lady in Afghanistan. It is not known, where in Afghanistan, she lives. Who is there in her family? Her hope and prayer read like this – "I live in an extremely challenging area in Afghanistan. My father was sympathetic to the Soviet force and always believed they could bring in peace and prosperity in my country. I was a little girl then.

He was killed by the terrorists. I did not have a choice for food, a good education. Somehow my mother managed to get a shelter. Still, my childhood was like a terror in my dream. Everywhere there had been mass devastation, cry for help. On one side, terrorists and extremists were threatening us. On the other hand, global forces were bomb-shelling our places to uproot the terrorists. I had a little child. He had a lot of dreams to change this country. I tried my best to give him the right education.

Two years back, bombshell took my son away forever. I never knew who did this. Was this the act of terrorists or was it carried out by the so-called global force? That day, I felt it was not just the death of a boy. I knew none in this world would know about it. But trust me, this death was like a loss of good soul on this planet and a winning situation for the evils. I am unfortunate to lose my father and son. Don't think I am broken. I am still strong, as a daughter, as a mother and a human being.

I would like to appeal to the wider world that nothing

could stop terrorism unless we all spend time, efforts and money to make the people educated, provide them good infrastructure to grow and prosper. There are many forces to brainwash innocent people and misguide them. Only when a good human extends the helping hand, the evil mind takes a back step. We need to remove all the darkness, bring people to the lights of education and prosperity. And the world could be rest assured that there won't be anyone left to join the hands to destroy our civilization."

Aakash received multiple comments from parts of Afghanistan, Pakistan and India. One aged person from a country in South East Asia wrote, "My father fought for the independence of united India. During the 1947 partition of India, we moved here. That time I was a little boy and am still in the dark why our united country and people had to break up? When I grew up, I started doing small business in a city here. I made my son very educated and he had his studies in a western country. When he came back, he became very different. He started talking about hatred for others. Not sure, how and where he had learnt all these things. Every night I go to bed with a nightmare of losing my son one day.

I know how the rest of the world looks at us, the people of my country. Yes, in the name of freedom fight some people may have supported extremists and terrorists. But that's not most people here. We have many people in this country who believe in brotherhood, peace and prosperity. Unfortunately, some leaders and powerful people don't want to stabilize the region. Instead of development, they are supporting acts against humanity. Multiple generations are being taught and routed to the wrong direction. We are losing the talent and youth in our own country. I hope one day we will have a great leader in the country, who will take us to the right path and show to rest of the world that we no more generate or support the terrorists, we can also generate the great sons of the soil."

Aakash was reading this comment and was thinking who says our neighboring country is all about extremism, hatred and terrorism. There are many great minds in that country as well. It is just that gradually these people are losing their dreams and voices like many other countries in the world. We can't let this dream die. Common people must come forward to save these great minds.

The other day, a gentleman in the defense service from a developed nation sent a note to Aakash. He said, "Aakash, I am so happy to read your blog. I am defense personnel. In the last 10 years, I have been on duty across various parts of the world. I have my wife and little son back in my country. Wherever there is a war against terror, we are posted there. I have seen so many places and met so many people in my decade-long career. Every time I go on duty, I can't come back before a year at least. I could never spend quality time with my family. When I see those children in Iraq and other golf countries, I remember my little son. Their faces tell me somewhere under the sky my son is smiling, playing with other kids. The women on the roads remind me that my wife is waiting for me at home. I am proud of my country. My life is dedicated to my nation. I only wish we don't need to get into 'war on terror' anymore. When will people leave this wrong way of looking at this beautiful world? I would rather like to come to these countries for disaster management, crisis management, and to help the people here. I am hopeful that day will come soon, and my own country will pave the path for that in the future world."

Aakash was overwhelmed to read the comments in his blog. The More he read, the more he got strength and belief that people around the world would act together to completely eradicate the root of terrorism. Many humans across the globe are hopeful to do that one day. If there are ten terrorists in this world, there are other ten thousand praying to end it.

Aakash met a young lady journalist from West Bengal, a few months back. She was travelling to Kashmir to do some research. She was highly educated, energetic and a dynamic personality. Aakash asked her, "Are you not afraid to travel in the valley alone?" The lady responded, "It's my country. They are my countrymen. Why should I worry?" She also recently commented on Aakash's blog. She wrote, "Aakash, I would be happy if you also come and join me in Kashmir. I am so excited to be here for the last few months. I know many people have the dream to see the Kashmir valley once in their lifetime. I am happy, I could make it. But I am even happier that I could meet so many nice people here. I could spend so much time seeing their daily lives, culture and challenges. You know, Aakash, after coming here I have started seeing the life from a different perspective. I was reaching out to all spheres of people. Some are educated, some not so educated, few rich, and many poor. They are Hindus, they are Muslims. Most of them are die-hard Indians. Few think it could be better to separate."

She continued, "Whatever differences they have, they have many common problems. Valley needs to be handled better. People need more access to education, modern technology, and affordable healthcare. People need better infrastructure for living. People here need jobs. The jobless youth think we're not thinking of them, and their future. Some of the people started believing that the government does not care for their misery. In fact, they are surprised that being a lady I have come here all alone to be part of their lives. They treat me like their daughter, sister and friend. I am so shocked to see that the same people throw stones at government offices, cars and government employees. I strongly believe, there are certain extremists who are making them feel that they are not part of India. We must stand by the people here, help them grow and prosper. We need to build many schools for children. The youth needs more job opportunities. There need to be more infrastructures for sports and culture. We must increase our people-to-people connections. If we show them the brotherhood, no separatist will be successful to divide us. The law and order need to be stronger. The theory of doubt needs to drop off and set examples to increase the trust."

After going through all such inputs from various parts of the world, Aakash remembered that childhood friend. He used to live in a small hut. His mother used to work as domestic help. And, his father was a daily laborer. Poverty made them live like animals. There was no respect, no education, no hope, and no identity. He used to say "I will earn lots of money one day, however bad way it could come. Then I will face this hypocrite society with the revenge". After two decades he is now living like a responsible citizen and an honest person. His motive in life has changed now to help others. Aakash does not know how this change could be possible. But it is a reality! I am hopeful, one day Kashmir will change as well.

Even if a percentage of people are derailed, we need to bring them back on track. Only way to stop any menace is to stop its spread. We need to ensure people get the basics of living. We need to ensure we include every facet of people in our journey. None should be left behind. If that calls for spending our entire defense budget into social welfare, so be it. If that means fighting 'war on poverty' instead of 'war on terror', so be it. We need to spread the waves of love, respect, and welfare for our people. Our country is heading in that direction. We are going to set examples before rest of the world that we can do it!

Empower Our Women...

We receive so much of love and affection from many women in our lives. It starts with mother and continues with grandmother, sister, sister-in-law, aunty, daughter, friend, wife and many others. They support us unconditionally all through our journeys. Our societies are so much thankful to the women, there is a popular saying, "Behind every successful man, there is a woman."

This is the 21st century and with more globalization, education, technology and freedom, women today stand as high as men in every other field. There are women, reaching the peak of The Everest, swimming across the English Channel, piloting planes across Atlantic and even going to space missions. They are great examples and very inspiring.

But this is not consistent in our society and doesn't represent the majority. Aakash's mother had always been a homemaker, whose whole life was dedicated to her family, be it, her in-laws, husband or the children. While she took care of the home for years, for every little thing she was always dependent on her husband. She did not have the financial ability to decide to buy a small cake or even ice-cream for her children, forget about good clothes or expensive toys. There are many women like Aakash's mother in our societies.

Aakash knew many women who were highly educated, worked for a couple of years and then became completely 'homemakers' to take care of the family and children. Many times, they are also humiliated and abused at home for asking even hundred rupees to buy something. Their fault is they do not earn money anymore. There are women across segments of our societies who are tortured days after days, just because they do not have financial independence and they are looked upon as feeble beings of the society.

We tend to forget or downplay their contribution to the family. Don't we feel how uncomfortable our lives become without these women in life?

The ugliest truth is that these women are so focused on family wellbeing, they forget their individual identities and many times, they even don't do justice to their own education and professional skillset. After two decades of serving their family, when their kids grow up and move to college or university or for the job, they start realizing they are not valued as much as they contributed. Women in general are very talented and are great managers. They run the family with so many different human beings, with much less budget than needed. They keep things ready for everyone in the family and that also consistently over the years. They sacrifice on their personal sides for bringing smiles to others. They never make us realize that we deprive them, for years, in fulfilling their aspirations.

A year back, Camellia had to go to Kolkata alone for some household work. It was just for 2 weeks. Aakash had to run the family along with his job. Every day, he had to wake up early in the morning, get Rayaan ready for school, prepare lunch for his son. Then Aakash would go to office, come back home in the evening and prepare the dinner. There was a lot of other work at home, be it cleaning the bed, floors, bathroom, and kitchen utensils.

There were many trees in his balcony that he had to take care of. He had to arrange for daily vegetables and food items and other household goods.

There were simply so many things to manage! In these two weeks, Aakash understood what it took to run a family. The good thing is when you focus on anything outside work, you don't get too much worried about just work. If you want to reduce work-related worries, start contributing at home. You will see it works like magic!

It is important we encourage women to learn new skills and focus on their passion. We need to facilitate them to be independent. If you see them good in certain skills, facilitate them to do even better. Camellia was very passionate about reading books, doing craftwork, and tailoring before her marriage. After marriage, Aakash discovered she has even interests in gardening, cooking new dishes. When Rayaan went to drawing classes, Aakash understood Camellia had a natural talent in drawing and painting. Aakash started facilitating her in each of these areas. He gave her a free hand to buy the books and journals she liked to read.

He bought a sewing machine for domestic purposes. He brought tubs and trees for Camellia to fulfil her gardening aspirations. Whenever he used to travel abroad, he used to bring new coins and currency notes for Camellia. Preserving these coins and notes had always been Camellia's hobby. Aakash also admitted Camellia in the fine art classes.

Camellia is a very confident lady today. She is now planning to run drawing and painting sessions as part of the 'Yatra' initiative. All Aakash did was to make her realize that she also had the skills to succeed. Camellia has not started earning yet, but Aakash is sure that she would be able to do that very soon.

Aakash also opened a bank account in the name of Camellia. Every month, the monthly household expenditure was deposited in that account for Camellia to manage the family independently. A small gesture from our side brings in so much of change in people's life.

We as a society won't flourish if women are left behind. We all need to encourage and facilitate them to be independent. We speak so much about inclusion and diversity in offices.

Let's walk the talk right from our homes. There are examples where women with a little bit of support and encouragement start helping other women to be self-sufficient. Women in our society have got tremendous skills and they just need to believe that they can do it. A famous physicist, Albert Bartlett said, "The greatest shortcoming of the human race is our inability to understand the exponential function." Once we all help each other to achieve a larger fit in life, the magic of exponential function keeps us wondering!

Globalization That We All Are Waiting For...

In the last couple of months, India has been witnessing a lot of unrest. The CAA, NPR and NRC have got their fame all over the world. At the same time, India now has one less state and two new Union Territories – Jammu and Kashmir, and Ladakh. We see a lot of well-wishers, trying their best to be on the side of common people through their own explanation of these issues. Representatives from various global bodies are visiting our country to assess the situation. Some people seem to be genuinely concerned, be it at home or outside.

We also had the honorable president of one of the largest democracies visiting our country. People of India gave him and his family a grand welcome. Two of the largest democracies in the world came even closer on the strategic front. Both countries are hoping to move on to a sustainable growth path based on mutual interest. It has been great to see two leaders are determined to go together to resolve various global issues. Energy and intent to make these two countries even greater are clearly visible.

The government of India and its people are committed to protecting the very secular characteristics of our democracy. We are the most diversified country with people from different spectrums of society, religion and belief, living together in harmony for years. There is no other country which is even closer to us in this aspect. There may be troubles in pockets, some people may not be in the mainstream. Some groups of people may continue to try to derail us. But we have many wise citizens to keep this country livable for all. Like the former US president Barack Obama said; it applies to our country as well, "Hope is the bedrock of this nation; the belief that our destiny will not be written for us, but by us."

My meeting with Aakash was an accident. His down-to-earth humble nature created a lot of curiosity in my mind. I spent a lot of time listening to his wishes, work and dreams. He made me believe that there are many people like him on this planet. Like his name (the sky), his presence is there all over. Aakash exists in many of us. Many societies are working towards fulfilling similar dreams. They are showing us the ray of light, leaving all the darkness behind. That is what keeps many of us motivated to express our minds through artistic work.

In last few decades, human has been extremely busy with technology innovation, infrastructure and the overall development. Some people have moved a bit ahead of others. The socio-economic state has created lot of imbalance in people. While we all love to see everyone accomplished and established, the hard reality has created walls between us. Inequality in society has become the biggest threat to mankind. Where do we start to fix this? How can we make our world more inclusive? Maybe that's why we need more people to dream and work. Who knows, maybe that day is not too far, when individuals, societies, nations will all work together to make this planet true heaven for human beings!

The great Mahatma Gandhi left a keynote for the future generation when he said, "If we want to reach real peace in this world, we should start educating children." Today's children are going to experience our future. We must create an environment where each human being will have equal opportunity to enjoy the basics of life – Food, Shelter, Healthcare and Education. Unless we try to bring all people into this basic humanity care net, we cannot reach the desired dreamland on this planet. Nelson Mandela had warned us long back, "When a man is denied the right to live the life he believes in, he has no choice but to become an outlaw." And the way to rectify this lies in one sentence, "What Can I Give?"

Thousands of years back, the human invented how to crop, how to fight with wild animals, etc. Everything was driven by the need for survival. We did not see the light of civilization yet. Still, we were united to face the challenges together. In between, during the journey, we forgot the fundamental truth that we are just another animal species on this planet with a superior brain. We started thinking of ourselves as different from the rest of the animals. And we moved further ahead and started differentiating between humans themselves. We started creating divisions, based on geographies, races, castes, languages, beliefs. During the early days of human civilization, we never had these differences. We only brought in the artificial boundaries amongst us. How can we expect that all human beings will behave in the same manner, with so much discrimination? We must take the oath to remove these differences and stay united! Once our children get the needed support, tomorrow's youth would be able to lead our society with a completely different perspective. The current generation of youth has already started showing tremendous potential. They are talented people and very thoughtful about basic expectations from a human. If their childhood is supported better, they can bring in the needed changes in our society. Greta Thunberg is just one example and there are many more across the globe. If we investigate all the good and bad sides of human civilization, people are at the center stage. It is the people who are spreading the waves of love, peace and harmony. For some bad incidents also, it is all about the people. Our society or nation is as good or bad as its people are.

Last century has achieved a lot in scientific and technical areas. All these accomplishments led to unmatched benefits to mankind. We wonder when we think, this has been possible with just a few percentages of people having access to food, education and home. Imagine a world, where we expand this creative population. What they all can contribute to larger social welfare is beyond our imagination! Today there are many children who don't get food, don't get an opportunity for education. Don't they have the right to dream just because they were born in a slum? When my kids, your kids are getting all that needed for them to grow, some children in the adjacent slum are struggling to get even a piece of bread? We hope our children will become someone one day with the kind of support we are providing them today. And those children? What will they do? If they choose the wrong route to maintain their livings, will we tag them anti-social? If we could track them to their childhood roots, it was dark all over, full of injustice, discrimination and struggle for survival. They were deprived, their childhood was deprived. More than their family, it is our own society, the government that should be blamed for injustice!

No society, nation is prosperous, civilized if there are people still struggling for education. No society, or a nation is safe if there are people fighting against poverty. Some established individuals, societies and nations may think they have moved forward. But for peace to rein in, they must be caring for those who are not so privileged. If people have education, food and shelter, if people are treated equally, why would they take arms to kill others? Darkness knows no differentiation. Only when there is a ray of light, the difference is visible, and one can choose between what is right and what is wrong! It is we who need to bring that light!

Lots of societies, corporate houses, non-government organizations are working across the globe to remove this difference. They are putting relentless effort to ensure children get access to primary education and basic health care. Many of them are inspired by what Mother Teresa used to believe – "Smile at each other. Smile at your wife, smile at your husband, smile at your children, smile at each other – it doesn't matter who it is – and that will help to grow up in greater love for each other."

We are one of the largest democracies in the world. We as a nation will be able to reap the benefits of democracies, only when our people are educated, aware and sensitive to widespread diversities that exist in our country today. We need to eradicate poverty to enable people to apply their democratic rights. If we can bring that balance in our society, we don't need to take the help of armed forces to conduct the elections. Light of education, awareness and financial freedom will make our people more disciplined. And disciplined people only know how to enjoy the greatness of democracy. The former US president Barack Obama said, "The role of a citizen in a democracy does not end with the vote." Our country must walk a few more miles even to realize the true democracy that starts with our vote. Of course, once we reach there, we will have bigger responsibilities to take our democracy to a larger height.

When we look at global issues, common people can only witness it. It is difficult to contribute and be a direct party in that process. Nobel laureate, Rabindranath Tagore inspired us saying, "You can't cross the sea merely by standing and staring at the water." We all need to act and act together to resolve all the issues the mankind is facing today. Aakash and similar individuals are part of that mission. We can contribute within our own space and when everyone does that, there is no room left for any discrimination. Mother Teresa said, "I look at the individual. I can love only one person at a time. I can feed only one person at a time. Just one, one, one."

In the end, what remains is humanity. Mahatma Gandhi used to believe, "You must not lose faith in humanity. Humanity is an ocean; if a few drops of the ocean are dirty, the ocean does not become dirty." Many organizations are deeply involved in sustainable development. Their focus is to ensure that development comes in an all-inclusive strategy. Every nation, every society must pay attention to the sustainable development model. And that model would be based on "Education for All", "Food for All", "Home for All", "Opportunities for All", "Freedom for All", "Security and Peace for All". There are many great individuals, organizations, and entrepreneurs, who are giving their best to bring in the balance in our society.

While those initiatives are getting more and more success gradually, few dark sides of human behavior, like "dishonesty", "corruption" are slowing down the progress. The great Dalai Lama taught us that "The world doesn't belong to the leaders. The world belongs to all humanity." That's where people like Aakash and his friends are trying their best to eradicate these human diseases from its root. If today's children are properly educated, they will teach their seniors one day that life is much beyond those small gains in life. There is a bigger target for us to chase and we can meet them through our genuine efforts, hard work and commitment. Whoever is achieving the certain target through corruption, will get their lessons from their children. Trust me; it will not be too far for those seniors to repent!

Few days back, I was traveling to another city. In the flight, there was a boy and his father, sitting beside me. It seemed the little boy was preparing for board examination in 10th grade. He asked his father, "Daddy, I see the maps and wonder how many counties there in this world are! Who created these boundaries? Why could not we just stay together?" I smiled at the boy. His daddy casually replied,

"The human did this. Why do you even want to know?" The child said, "I think it is not human, it is the rulers who built the borders". Then, he went on explaining that he has read lot of articles on the internet and found a few countries which even don't require any border between them.

I smiled at myself and decided to listen to that John Lennon music on my iPhone after a long time. Through the white cloud, the plane kept on rushing forward, while the earth became even more distant. The music took me to the cloud;

Imagine there's no heaven It's easy if you try

No hell below us Above us only sky

Imagine all the people living for today

Imagine there's no countries It isn't hard to do

Nothing to kill or die for And no religion too

Imagine all the people living life in peace, you

You may say I'm a dreamer But I'm not the only one

I hope someday you'll join us And the world will be as one…

We create a lot of borders, and not always just physical. There are borders almost everywhere. Few people created these borders for their benefits and the ease of ruling. And those borders are dividing us today brutally. More borders we create amongst us, more anger and unrest come into lives. In today's world, the west thinks east is not a place of development and prosperity. The east thinks west is trying to rule us through their economic and military might. No side is safe and secure until we treat every country equally. While some countries are fighting against poverty, lack of education, jobs; few others are trying to protect their countries, isolating the rest of the countries. The people staying in the underdeveloped nations are creating internal virtual borders based on religion and political beliefs. Darkness only leads to misery. That creates evil minds leading to mass destruction. Then the superpowers enter and try to control the situation through armed forces. This is the circle of everlasting misery!

Why spend so much on arms? Why to even sell mass destructive missiles to nations engaged in long-running wars? Does anyone believe that these wars would be limited to just one territory? Wars don't understand borders. They spread. They spread super-fast. When they spread, they can destroy everything that we have built over the decades. All the global powers must come forward and spend their money and efforts on humanity, not on wars. The future world is bound to move in that direction.

There won't be anything like my state, my country! It's human that matters the most. No world leader is a true leader unless they feel for the overall humanity. We have experienced these issues over the years, and we had our own learning. Dr. APJ Abdul Kalam had taught us, "LIFE and TIME are the world's best Teachers. Life teaches us to make good use of TIME and Time teaches us the value of LIFE."

There are certain things we, the common people can do and bring in the change that we would like to see. Societies and organizations are trying their best to bring a positive impact to millions of people. There are certain things that our political leaders must try to fix. In democracies, people vote for their leaders with lots of hopes and dreams. These elected leaders need to rise to the occasions and motivate the whole nation to build a better future for its citizens. In the last few decades, we have got many great political leaders. But the future world will look for more 'true human leaders. They will not just limit their vision hostage in their own territories. They will collaborate with other nations and make every attempt to bring in prosperity in common people's lives across the globe.

They would not be expected to create any new borders; rather they would break the borders for humanity. Imagine a day, when there is no border with our neighbors, and no armed forces needed to maintain peace. Imagine we don't need to spend so much money on defense and arms. Imagine our people have food, shelter, healthcare and education. Imagine we have plenty of jobs. Imagine none dies because of lack of food, medicines, political or religious riots.

All the challenges that the mankind is facing are mostly linked back to the downfall of humanity. Be it at home, in our society, office, nation; everywhere humanity has taken a back step. Few great minds are trying their best every day, every moment for the betterment of our living. They are our hopes. While the children are being taught the most difficult theory of science and mathematics, it is important to teach them the basics of humanity as well. We like so many posts on social media. We have built artificial intelligence to select the right profiles for a job. When would we have a humanity index for ourselves? The future world will require more human behavior than just technical skills and knowledge. We need to bring in a framework to recognize the great minds on the planet, uplifting the spirit of humanity. Any good act of humanity must be recognized and encouraged. The world is moving on the fast track and if humanity is left behind, we won't be able to sustain the overall development model.

Good news is, there are many beautiful minds, in the form of individual, society and nation in this world. It is they who are living our dreams through sacrifices. They represent us and they will bring in the changes, changes for a better world!

Journey Continues...

It was the beginning of the month of April. Rayaan's 10th grade board examinations were over. The little boy had finally got some relief. As planned before, Camellia, Rayaan, Aakash and his mother started for 2 weeks long trip through various places in West Bengal. They started with few temples, visited a couple of palaces in north Bengal and further moved north on their journey to the hill station of Darjeeling. In between, they stayed in hotels, took breaks, had tea and snacks from the roadside sellers. Every place they touched, it brought something new to them. On their way, they met many strangers. Music in the car, fresh air from nature and curiosity to see the next place kept the excitement on.

They spent a night in a hotel in Siliguri. The next morning, they started again through the jungles of Jalpaiguri. It would be a long leg of 4 hours of a drive at a stretch. All along, beauty was spread all over, as if someone had drawn a beautiful picture with a magical hand. Camellia and Aakash's mother were sitting at the back seats of the car. Camellia casually asked Aakash's mother, "Mother, you have seen a lot in your life. How do you assess your journey now? What is your view?"

Aakash's mother smiled and said, "Are you taking my interview?"

Rayaan looked back and prompted, "Grandmom, you have to share with us today. Otherwise, how would we know?"

Aakash opened the moon roof in his car. Fresh air and

sunlight came in. You could see the sky above. Grandmom did not have a choice. She started, “I never thought I would need to speak about this. Well, I was born in a family where we had many people around. We were seven siblings. I was never that interested in studies. My father arranged my marriage a bit early in a remote village. There was a lot of mismatch between people, in life in a city and a village. I saw how difficult it was for women to take a bath and go to the toilet. There was no electricity, no phone, no television. All I could see in the evening was darkness.”

Rayaan curiously asked, “Then? How did you adjust, grandmom?”

Grandmom paused and replied, “Life is the biggest teacher! We learn as we experience. Anyway, somehow, I got adjusted. It was a joint family. Income was not that good. Your grandfather tried his best to make everyone happy. Then we had three children. We could not give them many comforts in life. But they learnt to navigate through difficult times. We provided them real education, helped them to dream for future.”

She continued, “There was a time when it seemed just impossible to manage so many people with so little in hand. My children grew up. They were always the best of children; any parent could wish to have. They did well in their education, got good jobs. Gradually, our family in village shrunk with every death, and youngsters moving to cities for jobs.”

Rayaan got excited. He said, “Yeah, I heard a lot from daddy and mom. You had Tommy as well, right? I know about your brother’s story. Heard a lot about grandfather too”. He continued, “I am sure I missed all those experiences. Grandmom, are you happy with whatever you could achieve? What else you wanted to do and what is still pending?”

Aakash broke his silence, “Rayaan, let grand mom enjoy

nature. You are asking too many things." Camellia also nodded.

Aakash's mother said, "Let him know. He has every right to ask his grandmom." She continued, "Rayaan, I never believed in any target or accomplishment. I only wanted to make my family happy in whatever way I could. I wanted my children to be established one day and contribute to society in their capacity. Today when I look back, most of my dream has come true. I feel very proud of my family. My children are the best gifts for me. For me, the time has still paused there, when all of you gradually moved to other places. I hope you all will be coming there one day. For some time, we can go back to those golden times."

She continued, "I am confident my children won't live like ordinary people. They would always give their best for the society."

Rayaan could not stop himself. He said, "Now I understand what my dad always talks about. I get it now. Dad, the puzzle is resolved."

The car started climbing up the hills. Wherever they saw around, it was a tea garden. Aakash broke the silence and asked Rayaan, "Rayaan, won't you interview your mom? I am sure we need to know from her as well."

Camellia said, "I don't have much. I never had much of dreams or a special aspiration. I believe in simple living. I never take anything too seriously."

Rayaan joked, "Yes mom. That's why you take just a minute to sleep on the bed. But today, we would like to hear more from you. We will not leave you so easily. Grandmom, what do you say?"

Camellia responded, "See, after marriage, I mostly spent my life as a homemaker. I never had any personal priorities. Whatever priorities your dad had I followed that. Your dad had tried many things. At times, your dad did not achieve what he wanted. More than him, I felt the pain. His emotions and intent to do more for society has impacted us a lot. But I know that's what makes him happy. I have been always with him on his journey. That's what made our journey."

Rayaan smiled and said, "What's next mom? In two years, I will move to college. I am sure you will have more time to utilize."

Camellia with a pause responded, "Well, I have my plan. I would like to focus on smaller things in life. Maybe I will spend more time on painting; will travel to many places; will spend time with the kids in villages. Will do whatever I can do to contribute to society. I am sure your dad will have a bigger list. Who else will give him free support?"

Aakash's mother was hearing all these things. Now she asked Rayaan, "Rayaan, you are asking us so many things. What do you want to be?"

Rayaan jumped from his seat and prompted, "Grandmom, I am done. I have done everything that I wanted. Ahh…it was a joke. I am very lazy. I can't run behind things. I want to continue to learn physics. I believe all the mysteries in this world are hidden inside physics. I want to be a scientist and want to research in astrophysics. And finally, I want to work in a space research organization. That's what my professional goal is. On personal side, I want to change the way people see this world. I know dad always smiles when I say this. Of course, I want to see my parents happy with whatever I achieve in life. I will leave my scratch before I depart."

The car kept on running on. Aakash is very happy today. He could meet one of his long-cherished goals. When you have beauty all around, you just need a mind to feel it. Aakash once again understood the famous saying, "Nature is an infinite sphere of which the center is everywhere and the circumference, nowhere."

In the car, Camellia broke the seriousness and reminded Aakash that it was his turn now. He must speak his mind. They wanted to know what Aakash felt about his journey. Aakash's mother also insisted him to speak up. Aakash did not have a choice!

Aakash started with, "I know you will not leave me easily today and I have to say something. When I got my real sense during my early childhood, it was all about my parents, closed ones, Tommy, friends, neighbors, and teachers. It was a difficult journey in a village. But I was very fortunate. People around me inspired me to aspire. I was never the best student in studies, but I always aimed to be a good human. I always tried to be a good son, a good brother, a good friend, a good husband and a good father. In my professional career, wherever I worked, I had a sense of belongingness and I sincerely offered my best. When you set the yardstick for yourself, you just need to be better than you."

Everyone was listening to him. Aakash continued, "I dreamt to see a world with no differences between people. I wanted to see a world where every human being is respected; where there is no hatred for anyone. I wanted to see a world, where no one would be left behind."

Aakash took a deep breath and continued, "But you know what, time teaches us a lot. Soon I realized that we are very small creatures in this vast universe. Even the richest people cannot eradicate poverty completely. The wisest person cannot bring the light of education to everyone's life. The most loving person even cannot usher love to everyone. Changing the world is not one human's job. We can only do our part!"

None in the car wanted to stop him. Aakash continued driving and said, "I tried my best in my own capacity. But

I am too small in front of this large universe. I can dream a lot but can do very little about it. Then I realized the truth, the biggest truth in my life. We need to find happiness in smaller things. I realized what Mother Teresa meant when she said, "Not all of us can do great things. But we can do small things with great love."

Aakash was not sure who all were listening to him. He did not want to stop. He continued, "Whatever I am today, I am very happy about it. You want to know if I am what I wanted to be? Life does not have a constant journey; nor aspiration. There is nothing like being what we wanted to be. Rather we always try to be prepared with, what we want to be. Our inner souls only know what we have really achieved. We all can bring a lot of differences in our lives, in our societies. We can do small things with love. And together, that creates a massive positive impact on people's lives. Yes, we all can do that. No matter what, we should never compromise on humanity. All that our planet wants from us is simply humanity. The rest automatically follows. Whoever we are today, we are nobody unless we are good humans. Better be what you want to be".

Aakash continued, "You know, Rayaan, till the time our eyes get tearful seeing some misery, we are humans. I consider myself a human when I feel to stop my car on the road to help someone lying on the footpath without clothes and food. I am proud as a human when I give my best for those children who expect someone to bring smiles on their faces. I would consider myself human when I leave aside all my business and help an old person to cross that busy road. I feel I am human when I don't think twice to offer my food to someone starving."

Aakash continued, "I am sure there are many individuals who maybe doing even much bigger for the society. We can't just focus on ourselves and keep eyes closed from what is happening around us. If every blessed person can pull up another few people, mentor them, show them the right path, and be part of their journey, that's a great accomplishment."

Aakash looked at his son and concluded, "There would be a day, maybe tomorrow, maybe after a couple of years, maybe a decade, when you would see everything around you except your dad. If you would still feel proud of your dad that day, from a distant unknown place, I would feel to come down, meet you and say, "Yes, I am what I wanted to be!"

Music in the car was still on. Everyone was listening to the magical voice of Bob Dylan:

"How many roads must a man walk down
Before you call him a man?
How many seas must a white dove sail
Before she sleeps in the sand?
How many times must the cannonballs fly
Before they're forever banned?
The answer, my friend, is blowin' in the wind
The answer is blowin' in the wind."

After some time, Rayaan said, "let's take a break, as we continue with our journey. We still have a long way to go."

All sudden, there was the siren of an ambulance!

The Future Of Humanity Is In Our Hands...

The siren sound of ambulance broke Aakash's dream. Camellia had already started her day in the kitchen. Sunlight came through the window curtains. Aakash woke up. For a while, he sat in the balcony, staring at the clear sky. Since long they had planned for the trip to Darjeeling. They could not go. It remained only a dream. The situation had changed on the planet in the last one month. It is hard to differentiate between a dream and reality. Now, the dream has gone under the cover and reality is trying hard to bring it back.

Back in February-March, the world heard about this; the coronavirus disease, an infectious disease caused by a newly discovered coronavirus. It infected people in one country and gradually started spreading in other countries. In a month's time, it became a pandemic. Millions of people are impacted; more than two hundred thousand people have already died. The number kept on soaring with every other day. Scientists across the globe are trying their best to find treatment and are yet to share the good news. It is not yet known how long it will take to find a medicine or vaccine. People started social distancing to avoid the spread of this disease. All global cities have got into a state of lockdown. Something invisible has challenged mankind brutally. Something invisible has shaken us up, alerting all to act; fight together and save humanity!

Much before this pandemic, there were many problems. Poverty itself has limited the ability to realize mankind's full potential. Lack of education and healthcare services impacted many countries. And still, many societies had not experienced the blessings of equality and inclusion. Environment and climate have been badly impacted due to devastating pollution. Arms and wars had kept many countries away from true human living. Terrorism became the biggest enemy of humanity. Corruption had made many countries almost disabled. More the globalization, bigger has been the gap between humans in the name of 'survival of the fittest'. Humans assumed to act like 'superpower' and started molding the world from all corners. Miseries did not find a cause to end. Somewhere humanity covered its face!

With all these odds, humans still exist. Civilization continues to move on. On one side, we have seen the most shameful acts of humans. At the same time, many individuals, societies and nations have shown us how to protect our basic values. Despite many challenges, they are making this world a better place to live. Be it scientific development, technology innovation, social revolution, or human rights protection – they are our hopes; our superheroes. They are the reasons; we still love to live.

What has happened in the last three months is unprecedented. Everywhere in the world, there is a loss of lives. Many business houses and offices had to be temporarily closed. People across the globe have got into self-imprisonment. Lockdown took the lives some decades back, with very few people appearing in our vision. Even in the most developed nations, people are so helpless to cope up with the situation. The countries with the best medical infrastructure are struggling to find a response in the face of coronavirus. We were not at all prepared to face this widespread challenge. It is as if some magician has changed the known planet. And, some unseen creature has instructed people to hide behind.

While some sections of people are comparatively better

placed, many people are struggling to cope up with the situation. Many migrant workers are stranded in pockets. Poor people are walking hundreds of kilometers to reach their native places. Daily laborers are uncertain about when they can work again. How long will people continue to struggle? How many of them will be able to face this challenge? The situation is common across the globe. We see the helpless faces on television and the internet every day. There are children, old and young. Some are men, some women. Some are white and some black. They are Hindus, Muslims, Christians. They are Indians, Chinese, Russians, Germans, Americans. But, above all they are humans. Everywhere it is a struggle, struggle to live one more day!

Difficult time brings the best of humans. We see government bodies are highly proactive. Professionals like doctors and caregivers are putting their lives at risk to save others. Police and security guards are awake on the roads to keep us safe at home. Scientists are having sleepless nights to discover medicines. Media personnel is putting relentless effort to keep us posted on the latest happenings. It's heartening to see so many people are putting their hearts and souls for humanity. Earth required a reason to unite people and bring back humanity. However evil it is, coronavirus could be one such messenger!

Nature also renewed itself. The level of pollution has decreased to a large degree. After a long time, we see those birds and animals back to our localities. We all have a longer, clear vision now. Water in rivers is much clearer. Air is much fresher to inhale. Trees have got their leaves greener, with colorful flowers. Nature is refreshing itself, while humans are witnessing everything silently from inside the home. We have re-discovered how beautiful our nature could be.

In difficult times, new heroes are born; new leaders step in. They are individuals, societies with the real face of humanity and serving people selflessly. The pandemic has revealed to us, there are so many people, who are doing above and beyond the limitations to support the fellow citizens. Social distancing has bonded people together through self-discipline. The face of humanity that was lost somewhere is back again. There are real examples of individuals who are making 'larger than life' impact on our societies.

When did we last come out of our houses to pay respect for medical professionals? When did we last feel to offer food to our community security personnel? When did we last see a local leader, herself spraying disinfection liquid into her locality? When did we last see an old woman offering her ventilator to another young patient saying, "I have lived my life enough"? When did we last see IT professionals making masks to help common people? When did we last see a child giving all his savings to policemen for supporting the war against coronavirus? When did we last see rich people going to the slums with food packets? SALUTE to these individuals! WE ARE PROUD OF YOU ALL!

The pandemic revealed, there are many 'Aakash' in our societies across the nations. They are there with different names and identities. They are amongst us everywhere to rise to the occasions and create a positive impact on our lives. The world has come together after a long time to fight it out. Major differences have been forgotten now. The fight against coronavirus continues. The journey to bring back humanity has started!

When I met Aakash and his family, his dream and efforts to realize it deeply touched my heart. Being a common ordinary man, he did not stop with small barriers. Every morning he wakes up with a zeal of touching the lives of many other people. He and many of his friends and near ones are determined to make a difference. I tried to witness everything they tried. Their effort is real and truly priceless, inspiring to many of us.

But Aakash is just another person. There are many others who are also on similar missions. With limited capacity, they may not create impact on wider segments of our societies or nation. But their efforts in every small circle set example before us. Their determination and commitment motivate us. Good work always spreads, touches the hearts of many others. Their every effort inspires others to do more.

We have a much bigger battle to fight in the coming days. While we pray for medicines, we must prepare ourselves to fight a longer battle against coronavirus. We may experience even worst days in the near future. That's when we will need to stand in solidarity to protect humanity above anything else. I am not sure where exactly on this planet, Aakash and his friends are having the battle now. But thousands of 'Aakash' will show us how to remain human even in the darkest world. While corporates, governments and nonprofit organizations continue to extend their helping hands, common people will have very critical roles to play. Each 'Aakash' in the society must form a virtual 'chain of ten'. Every member of the chain needs to be taken care of during the difficult times. If some of us can take care few others in our circle, no one will be left alone in this journey. Nothing should derail us from our mission to uplift humanity. We must continue to share the pain together. Nobody should be left behind. The virtue that is back in our life, we must not let that go again.

And then a day will come, people will win the battle against coronavirus, humanity will have the last smile. The whole world will celebrate the victory together, maybe for the first time in the history of the world. We must not forget what we are witnessing in this coronavirus episode. We must break all the walls that we have built artificially between us. Instead of arms and wars, we will spend our money to keep nature intact. We will rather focus on true development. We will work together to build an inclusive society, a truly global society. I am sure there will be thousands of 'Aakash' on that journey all over the world. The history of mankind would be rewritten after a few decades. Money and power alone won't rule that world. Humanity will define the new way of living and sense of accomplishment on this planet. Together, we can build a better world for us!